THE DUALITY PRINCIPLE

REBECCA GRACE ALLEN

This is a work of fiction. Names, characters, places, and incidents are the product of the author's imagination or are used fictitiously. Any resemblance to actual events, locales, or persons, living or dead, is purely coincidental.

Rebecca Grace Allen Enterprises

The Duality Principle

Copyright © 2014 by Rebecca Grace Allen

Print ISBN: 978-0-9978792-9-2

Digital ISBN: 978-0-9978792-3-0

Editing by Christa Soule

First Samhain Publishing, Ltd. electronic publication: November 2014

CONTENTS

Sometimes opposites do way more than just attract...

Wild passion is a luxury PhD candidate Gabriella Evans can't afford. Her career needs her complete focus. And the ridiculously sexy tattooed biker she's seen on the streets of her small coastal town is very distracting. But giving in to her reckless, rebellious desires would be a huge mistake...right?

Connor Starks gave up his bad boy ways long ago. These days, he'll do whatever is necessary to be a better man. But with Gabriella, everything is harder. Literally. Eventually, he's afraid he'll lose control. And if he does, she'd better hang on tight, because it's going to be a rough, dirty ride...

Can these polar opposites find their way to happily ever after? Only if the ghosts of Connor's past—the ones that refuse to stay hidden—don't ruin everything first...

The Duality Principle, book 1 in the Portland Rebels series, is a steamy summer romance featuring a nerdy heroine and a reformed bad boy finding their HEA...with a little spanking and outdoor sex along the way. Grab a glass of ice water (you'll need it) and grab it today.

The Duality Principle. (dü′al·əd·ē ′prin·sə·pəl)

A principle that says if a theorem is true, it remains true if each object and operation is replaced by its dual.

Rebel. (′rebəl) Noun.

A person who resists rules or norms.

Defiant, disobedient.

Unruly.

Subverts authority, control, or tradition.

ONE

G abriella Evans's life existed in terms of definitions.
She studied algebra, geometry and calculus—concepts
that were ordered and well-defined. Logic was where she felt
most comfortable, so she couldn't understand why she'd
abandoned her research for the afternoon and was instead about
to go on a blind date. It was the least logical thing she could
possibly do. The whole thing had a seventy percent chance of
being completely awful. She could have written an entire thesis
on the statistical probability of a blind date going well. Still, it was
nice to be out in the sunshine, enjoying the town she loved.

Portland, Maine sat amidst the backdrop of the sparkling
Atlantic Ocean, still frigid despite the balmy air. Lobster buoys
and white sails dotted the coastline, making it a spot of serenity
only two hours up I-95 from Cambridge. All around her, the Old
Port was filled with the usual invasion of tourists competing for
space with the locals. They wandered through the cobblestoned
streets, past the art galleries and quaint stores selling kitchen
knick-knacks. Children pressed their sweaty palms against ice
cream parlor windows while college students played guitar on the

sidewalks. Colorful windsocks hung from awnings outside bohemian clothing shops, whispering in a breeze laced with the scent of salt water.

These people, these sights, sounds and smells—they were home to Gabriella, so much more than the rigid life in Boston where she'd grown up. She was sure the sleepy town where she spent the carefree summers of her youth would be the perfect place to evaluate her thesis statement and plan for her last year of study. She was in Portland to do research. Not to go on a blind date.

She never should have let Jamie talk her into this.

Gabriella glanced at her watch, even though she didn't need to check the time. She was always early. Always on time, always routinized, everything in her life perfectly ordered. Except for her heart.

"I don't want to do this," she complained to her wrist.

The couple to her left turned to stare at her, their eyebrows raised in unison. Gabriella smiled awkwardly before quickly moving away. Talking out loud was a bad habit she'd developed at M.I.T.—a habit that textbooks and numbers didn't seem to mind but wasn't exactly considered normal among the general public.

She stopped at the crosswalk, a safe distance away from her embarrassment. The early summer sun washed brightly over her bare shoulders, and she reached up to twist her hair into a rope at the nape of her neck, hoping for some relief from the heat. Never one for fashion, because who had time to care about that when you're busy trying to disprove archaic theories, Gabriella didn't bother to style her hair. She always let the locks dry on their own, relying on the laws of entropy to decide her look for the day.

She knew she didn't appear like the stereotypical mathematics PhD candidate. While her black-rimmed glasses provided her with the typical nerdy girl image, she had strong legs from years of hiking, a flat belly, and enough cleavage to fill her C-cup bras. There was a lot more to her than math—she'd always thought of herself as a kind of sexpot rebel behind the glasses and numbers. Not that any of her boyfriends had ever noticed that.

Gabriella let go of her hair and brushed her fingers over the piercing on the inner flap of her ear. She'd done it to stand out from her peers, with their ability to become borderline-orgasmic after writing a pristine mathematical proof. She'd been tempted to get piercings in her nose and eyebrow too, but that would have meant having to remove them whenever her parents came to visit. Thank God they'd never know about the tattoo.

She'd gotten the ink done in another moment of rebellion. Unzipping her jeans in a seedy shop in Harvard Square, she'd revealed the bare patch of skin where her thigh met her pelvis for the artist's needle. There she was, the straight-A student, the future Fields Medal hopeful, getting a tattoo inches away from her crotch. It felt like such a triumph to rise up against the idea of who everyone expected her to be. The image drawn onto that illicit spot was like a tiny piece of armor, a secret middle finger held up to the mold she was supposed to fall into.

The cars on Commercial Street slowed to a stop, the break in the traffic allowing her to cross. She'd just stepped off the curb when the sharp buzz of a motorcycle's tires spinning against the asphalt tore through the serene New England quiet. Gabriella stopped short as the bike fired down the road at a speed surely reserved for the Autobahn and screeched to an abrupt halt less than a yard away from her. She should have barked at the reckless asshole in front of her, yelled out something about being careful and who the hell did he think he was, but all she could do was stare. The rider in the black leather jacket, gloves and helmet with the opaque pane was someone she'd seen before. Someone she'd fantasized about before.

Ever since the first time she heard the roar of that bike, all danger, exhaust and breakneck speed, the man riding it had haunted her thoughts. She couldn't count how often she imagined the sweaty body underneath all that leather, dressed for the road even in the heat. She'd never had a thing for bikers before, but there was something about him, something that made her sex drive sit up and take notice. There were plenty of weekend warriors that rumbled through the streets of Portland in summer, but they always appeared in bearded swarms, rolling into town like slow-moving locusts.

Her rider always rode fast, and he was always alone.

She hurried across the street, feeling his eyes on her, tracking her like heat. He always did that, whenever they crossed paths. His helmet would turn slightly, just enough to give the impression that he was following her moves. It made her skin come alive somehow, a chill that slid down her spine straight to the apex below her tattoo, slick places where she was empty and aching.

When she'd safely stepped onto the opposite curb, she turned in time to watch his hand twist over the handlebar. The powerful beast beneath him growled, but he held it back. Gabriella wondered if he could tame *her* into submission too. If one flick of his wrist would make her bow to his every whim, her body following where he led.

After one last pause, he revved the bike's engine and sped away, turning off Commercial Street and out of her sight. She stared after him and frowned as the sounds of his recklessness faded into the distance. It tugged at her in ways she didn't like, this curiosity about who he was. Her infatuation had prompted her to ask Jamie, her neighbor and childhood friend, about him. Jamie grew up in Portland, with a popularity and natural social grace Gabriella would have killed for. She knew everyone, and so Gabriella had tried to mimic Jamie's poise, studying her nails as she asked about her rider's identity. But when Jamie asked why she was interested with a grin, she thought better of it and dropped the subject. Admitting that she was lusting after some stranger on a bike was not happening, to herself or to Jamie.

Which begged the question of why she was still staring in the direction of his disappearance.

She whirled around and faced the other way.

"Get a grip, Gabriella. You're here to go on a blind date, not stare at men on motorcycles."

She clamped her lips shut as soon as she spoke, tallying up her bad habits in her head: talking out loud and lusting after a man on a bike. Both of them needed to stop. Particularly the talking. If the cops picked her up for appearing criminally insane, her parents would be humiliated.

Then again, she'd actually have to be talking to them for that to happen.

Communication had become something she found completely useless after they told her they were selling Nana's house. She could have tried to reason with them, to explain that they were selling part of her soul, but what would have been the point? Things had already been strained between them since her breakup with Kevin.

Kevin was an engineering student, a promising husband in the making who also happened to need a detailed topographic map to find her clit. Gabriella chose not to share that particular bit of information with her mother when she gave them the bad news during her last visit home.

"I thought Kevin would last at least a little bit longer than the others," her mother had complained. "You're never satisfied. How will you get a husband if you keep breaking up with every single one?"

Gabriella didn't bother to explain that she wasn't willing to spare her free time settling for the monotonous conversation and lackluster orgasms Kevin had to offer. Instead, she'd stayed quiet during the lecture, mimicking her father. He sat across the table from her, distant as always, his eyes barely skirting over the edges of his newspaper.

"Your grandmother wanted to see you married before she died, you know."

It had been a low blow for her mother to bring up Nana like that—the only person who made Gabriella feel like she was enough, without credentials at the end of her name, or a husband changing the prefix before it.

She didn't reply, but did hazard a glance at her father to see if the mention of his late mother had broken through his implacable exterior. The newspaper had remained a crisp barrier between them, and the rest of the meal had passed in silence.

Gabriella curled her fingers into determined fists and forced herself to walk toward the café. Dating, like her mother's expectations, was something she'd hoped to avoid this summer, but Jamie's chastisement from a week ago still echoed in her head: "You're spending the whole summer alone in your dead grandmother's house. Come on, live a little!"

It was the usual dry style of encouragement she'd learned to expect from her friend. Gabriella could only ignore Jamie for so long before she hit critical overload. It didn't help, of course, that Jamie was right. So she'd agreed to be set up with Connor Starks, a classmate of Jamie's from South Portland High. He was twenty-four years old, the same age as her, tall with brown hair and blue eyes, and was a programmer of some kind. There was nothing about Jamie's description that should have given her a sense of foreboding. However, before she even left the house that afternoon, she believed that this date, like all the others she had before, was doomed.

They always started the same way, with pleasant conversation about their majors and plans of study. Just like Gabriella, her dates would be up to their ears in schoolwork and barely had time to breathe, let alone have a relationship. Still, coffee would eventually turn to dinner, dinner to a movie in between their research and lectures, and a movie to tame sex that got the job done but still left her wanting. Time after time, it drove her bat shit crazy.

After a few laps in bed, the lights off and the covers forming an air-tight tent over their bodies, she'd suggest something a bit wilder. Maybe some dirty talk. A little hair pulling. A spanking would have been hot too. If she was feeling particularly bold, she'd bring up wanting to do it in public places on campus. By the research stacks in the library. Or in one of the stairwells at the lab. It was cliché, but it was such a turn-on to think of getting naked in the hallowed halls of the country's premier school of math and science.

Without fail, her dates would respond with the same disapproving and occasionally even fearful looks that seemed to say, "You're too much of a freak for me, Gabriella Evans." She'd cringe inwardly and recant, hiding her embarrassment and frustration by saying it was just a joke. Inevitably, every short relationship would end with her feeding the guy one of the same lines:

I just don't feel the same way.

I have to focus on my studies.

Or simply, *I'm sorry.*

She'd used all three with Kevin, and since breaking up with him, Gabriella had given up. It was time for her to box up her wild side. To lock it down and throw away the key. A surefire way to fend off the sting of rejection was to simply stop expressing her desires and, ideally, to stop feeling them altogether. She had to— the things she craved in bed were completely the opposite of how she acted in life, in her studies and in her future career. She should have been above her baser instincts. She was too liberated, too ordered, too logical to yearn for a fist in her hair, to have her ass slapped, to be taken hard and fast in places she could so easily get caught.

No, she couldn't think that way anymore. That was part of the reason she'd holed herself up in this little town for the summer, in her grandmother's empty seaside cottage. She needed to get her head on straight. To find the proof that she couldn't be both a successful mathematician and crave the wanton, dominating, careless bad boy.

But she did.

She couldn't help it. She didn't want sweet, intelligent and safe. She wanted more. She wanted a man who would let her lose control—no, who would *make* her lose control. To have a presence so commanding and use words so filthy that she was too turned on to think or see straight. It was a need she felt at her pulse points, rushing through her blood. She'd tried to fight her cravings with reason, but there were no theorems to help discount the fact that she wanted a man who could make these fantasies a reality.

Pausing as she neared the coffee shop, Gabriella thought about her rider. She couldn't put her finger on why he intrigued her so much, but whenever he flew down the street, wheels ripping through the quiet, he became the embodiment of everything wild and untamed, the center of all her fantasies without ever showing his face. Every time his visor-hidden eyes tracked her movements, she wished he would follow her down a wharf somewhere, advancing on her like something primal and dangerous, lust in the form of a leather jacket and jeans.

The recurring fantasy she'd had all summer began again. She'd hear the sound of the bike first—that buzz of his engine and the streak of rubber across concrete that made her insides leap and twist. Next he'd pull up in front of her house, disembark from the bike and advance toward her, one slow step up the porch at a time, staring her down with a purpose that would make her tremble. Then he'd back her up against the wall and kiss her hard.

He'd be the one to take her how she'd always wanted. He'd fist her hair and bite her neck, all grit and sweat and dirty words in her ear. He'd fuck her to a violent orgasm, so swift in intensity that it was almost painful, and then do it again and again and again.

Gabriella groaned. These fantasies had to stop.

She shook her head free of the daydream, pressed her palm against the cool glass door to the coffee shop where she was supposed to be in approximately eight minutes, and went inside.

TWO

The café was fairly empty for the Saturday before July fourth. Gabriella found a table easily, one in the corner by the front window. It was the perfect spot to observe all the men who came in, thankful each one was not her date. The first was a straggly, bearded redhead with a skateboard under his arm. Next a tanned blond wearing the tourist's uniform of an L.L. Bean baseball cap and a Mountain Tops T-shirt, followed by one with a shaved head and a handlebar mustache.

Then Connor arrived.

It had to be him. There was no mistaking Jamie's description, but "tall with brown hair and blue eyes" barely did him justice.

She ducked down, pretending to diligently examine the menu as she watched him. Connor was easily over six feet tall, with chin-length, silky hair he'd unsuccessfully attempted to comb neatly back. It curled up under his ears, a look that was both adorable and sexy. His face was pretty damn close to perfect, clean-shaven with a tiny cleft at the base of his chin. He was broad too, like a lumberjack beneath his boxy button-down shirt and khakis. He looked so sturdy, like he could chop down a tree with his bare hands, carry the wood home and build a house for her out of it. And when he finally canvassed the corner she was sitting in and met her gaze, a boyishly handsome widening of his eyes set off a spark in her belly.

Then she noticed the phone attached to his belt loop, in a sturdy case worthy of a Storm Trooper, and she knew right away that Connor was another sweet, nerdy boy who was going to bore the crap out of her.

"Gabby Evans?"

She opened her mouth, prepared to correct him and insist that he call her Gabriella like everyone else did, but stopped. No one but Nana ever called her Gabby. It felt good to hear the nickname again.

"That's me," she said. "I assume you're Connor Starks?"

Connor leaned back a touch, his brow pushed down in what looked like confusion. But he recovered quickly, features evening out as he flashed her a smile.

"I am. It's nice to meet you." He pulled out the chair across from hers and sat down. He was so tall that his knees just barely skimmed the bottom of the table. "So what are we having?"

Connor flipped through the menu, pursing his lips together as he read. Gabriella watched his mouth, studying it like a test object in a lab. There was a little indentation above his upper lip, and for some reason she couldn't help wondering how soft it must be. She wanted to reach out and dip her finger into it.

Only to verify her hypothesis, of course.

"I'm happy with just decaf," she said.

"Well, I'm starving. I'll have coffee too, and a piece of strawberry shortcake." He glanced up at her. "If you'd like to share."

Gabriella didn't answer at first, because eating would make this take longer than she'd planned, and nothing said awkward like sharing food with a complete stranger. It was also three in the afternoon—that weird hour too late for lunch and too early for dinner—but she could withhold judgment on the date's outcome for a little bit longer. Plus, she was hungry. Cake sounded good.

"Sure," she replied.

He grinned at her, a mischievous gleam in his eyes as he flagged down the waitress.

Connor turned away from her to order, but his smile echoed in her vision. It wasn't so much a smile, but a smirk that left a pulse of heat behind in its wake. It was lopsided, curling up to one side a little more than the other. His cheek curved with the lines around it, his lips ridiculously full and pink. While his face may have been boyish, and his cell phone case screamed geek in a way that made her want to cringe, that smile of his was dangerous. It made her wonder if there was anything else about him that wasn't as cookie-cutter as he seemed.

The waitress quickly delivered their coffees. Connor took a sip from his, and a droplet remained behind, settling into that adorable little dip. He licked it—an absent-minded slide of his tongue across his upper lip. The sight drove a surge of lust in between her thighs.

It wasn't because of him. It was simply because of how long it had been since she'd felt anyone's tongue there in a way that didn't make her stare at the ceiling and count the tiles until enough time passed that she could fake her orgasm.

"Well, I've got to say I'm really relieved," Connor said, shaking her out of her thoughts.

"About what?"

He leaned in toward her and crossed his arms on the table. "That Jamie was telling the truth. She usually exaggerates about everything."

"That's frighteningly accurate. What was she actually honest about this time?"

"That you're really pretty."

Her cheeks defied her in a heated rush of pink. She glanced away, hiding her face and mumbling a thank you.

"You're welcome." Connor's speech slowed, his gaze sweeping her cheeks appreciatively before he rocked back in his chair. His massive shoulders almost eclipsed the back of it. "Admit it. You were a little nervous about this too, right? I mean, the probability of a blind date working out is practically zero."

Thirty percent, Gabriella thought, but she didn't want to correct him. He deserved credit for trying.

She offered him her best sarcastic grin. It would be fun to tease him a little, just to see what happened. "What makes you so sure this one is working out already?"

Connor smiled down at his cup. When he looked back up at her again, his eyes were hooded with lashes longer than anyone over six feet should have. He raised one dark eyebrow.

"So far so good, right?" He softened his voice a notch when he said it too.

"So far."

She had to give him that much. He'd earned himself a few points at least for the smirk and the eyebrow. The gorgeous face didn't hurt, either.

Connor cleared his throat. "So Jamie said you're a grad student?"

"Yup. Seems I couldn't get enough of M.I.T. after four years there as an undergrad, so I decided to just keep going to school rather than face the big bad world." That made Connor grin again, but his eyes were fixed on her, reminding her a little of the focused way last year's freshmen had watched her when she'd given lab instructions as a TA. "I'm in the Applied Mathematics PhD Program there. I'll be starting my final year in the fall."

"So all you do is...math?"

Gabriella rolled her eyes.

"Well, I don't sit around just *counting* things all day," she drawled, and his smile grew wider. God, even his teeth were white and perfect. "The program covers tons of stuff: probability, astrophysics, fluid dynamics, number analysis. We take courses in engineering and science too. And if my thesis gets accepted for publication, it could mean some big things for my career."

She only noticed she was babbling when she caught the way Connor was looking at her. This time his lips were pressed into an amused stance, like he was trying not to laugh.

"That all sounds pretty intense." His smile was kind, but her face heated again nonetheless.

God, since when had anyone made her blush like that?

"It is."

Intense didn't even begin to cover it, but she didn't want to say more and risk having her mouth run away with her again.

"Hmm." Connor's mouth twisted to the side, as if he were considering her answer. "So obviously all things mathematical take up most of your time. What do you do for fun?"

The question caught her off guard. Her dates didn't usually ask her that. As a matter of fact, she couldn't remember one of them keeping their eyes on her for so long without taking a break to check their email.

"You mean studying fluid dynamics and numerical analysis doesn't sound fun to you?" she asked.

This time, he did laugh, a chuckle that was low and sultry. The sound did something to her it had no business doing.

"Oh, it sounds like a blast, all right. But there's got to be something you do to blow off steam."

Telling Connor the things she fantasized about doing to "blow off steam" was definitely not first date material. But maybe it wouldn't hurt to be honest about other things.

"I hike a lot, when the weather's nice," she told him. "I like being outside, in nature."

"Smart *and* outdoorsy." Connor cocked his head and pointed

at the right side of her face. "I wouldn't think a girl so into numbers would have a bit of spunk to her."

It took her a minute to figure out that he meant her earring, and she fingered it without thinking.

"Well, like I said, I don't just study numbers. I'm actually working on disproving a theory."

"Which theory is that?"

"It's called the Duality Principle."

Gabriella paused, sure he wouldn't be interested in any of the mundane details, but Connor inclined his head, silently bidding her to go on.

"The Duality Principle says that if a theorem is true, it remains true if each object and operation is replaced by its dual. In math, that means given one conclusion, we can easily reach another one which is equally important. Duality is the quality of being two-fold, so if something is true, it remains true if it is replaced by its dual, or its opposite."

She was babbling again. The same amused grin was back on his face.

"Yeah, I didn't understand a word of that."

She half cringed, half laughed. Having to explain things was another break from the status quo. Most of her dates were already familiar with what she studied, turning romantic candlelit evenings into debates. This was a nice change of pace.

"Sorry. It's just a fancy way of saying that two things that are the same can be interchanged without changing the result."

"It seems pretty complicated."

"It's not that complex, but it also happens to be completely preposterous and I am going to bring it down."

"Do you have a personal vendetta against duality?"

"I don't. I just think it makes no sense."

"Why?"

"One entity, capable of being two completely different things?" She shook her head. "It's not possible."

Connor's eyes were still on her when the waitress arrived with their plate of cake. He thanked her for it and picked up his fork before nodding at Gabriella. "Do you want the first bite?"

"You go for it."

He looked at her a moment longer and then slowly sliced his fork sideways through the tender shortcake and whipped cream. It was somehow ridiculously erotic. She didn't realize she was staring until he lifted a morsel of the dessert from the plate and raised it to her mouth instead of his own.

"Ladies first. I insist."

It wasn't offered easily, though. He held the fork just far enough from her mouth so that she would have to lean in to bite the dessert from it. He was making her work for it, beckoning her closer. She smiled at the challenge and held his stare, tilting forward over the table until she could steal the piece of cake with her teeth. She sat back and bit down, savoring the taste. The satisfied grin on Connor's face as he watched her swallow made her belly flare.

The door to the café opened and closed, the little bell attached to it breaking the mood. Connor blinked and frowned at his plate. He looked suddenly uncomfortable and busied himself with taking a long sip of his coffee. Gabriella sliced a mouthful of the dessert with her own fork. It tasted better when Connor fed her, which, of course, made no sense at all.

"So you're a computer programmer?" she asked, uneasy with the silence.

"Yeah. I work at a local web marketing firm."

"What do you do there?"

"I code stuff."

He gathered another piece of cake for himself. When he bit it off the fork, he caught her watching and smiled around the utensil, pulling it slowly back out of his mouth.

Gabriella took a breath. It was annoying, to be jealous of a piece of silverware.

"Is your degree in computer engineering?" she asked, forcing herself to concentrate on something other than his mouth.

Connor's expression changed, blanking out, shutters rolling down on his smile. "I took some classes in it, but I pretty much taught myself all I know."

He didn't offer any more information. Gabriella tried to analyze the situation. Did he switch majors, or did he get a degree in something else and make a career change at the last minute?

"Are you staying in town with family for the summer?" he asked, clearly changing the subject. Gabriella didn't like not having answers to her questions but let it go anyway.

"Not really, no. I mean, I'm staying at my grandmother's house, but she passed away. Last fall."

Lines creased his forehead. "I'm sorry to hear that."

She nodded and smiled, fighting back the sting of tears.

"It's okay," she said, even though it wasn't. "She died peacefully in her sleep. And I love being in her house." A house that she would be losing soon. "It reminds me of her and how it felt to be a kid when I'd come here in the summers. It's off the cove, right by the water. That's how I know Jamie. She's my neighbor."

She didn't know why she was telling him all that. This wasn't the time to break down about Nana, or the house, or how her parents were hell-bent on selling it.

"I didn't know that. I live a few blocks away from you."

"Really?" The seacoast area wasn't cheap. "Did you buy something, or do you rent?"

He drummed his fingers against the table, his mouth opening and closing, like he'd realized he'd offered too much information and wasn't sure what to say next. "Actually, I live with my grandparents."

That wasn't the answer she'd expected. She wanted to know more, but then the waitress dropped the check on the table. Connor snatched it up and pulled his wallet from his back pocket. Gabriella reached down to rummage through her bag, but by the time she'd touched her own wallet, he was waving the waitress back and handing cash over to her.

Kevin had always insisted on going dutch, calculating each of their shares down to the penny.

"Thank you," she said.

"My pleasure." Connor focused his attention on putting his wallet away, eyes averted. "So maybe we can go out again? How about ice cream, at the place on the corner of Wharf Street? I'm free on Wednesday."

"Maybe." She wasn't agreeing to anything yet. Logically, there was no reason she should. The statistical thirty percent remained. The date could still go sour.

Connor smiled down at the table then gave a swift scan around the café. An errant strand of hair fell over his forehead. He looked back at her and nodded to the plate between them. It had one lone piece of cake on it.

"You want the last bite?"

This time his smile was innocent, but the look in his eyes was anything but.

"Sure."

Gabriella reached for her fork, but Connor held up his hand to stop her. Capturing the remaining bit of cake between his thumb and forefinger, he brought it up to her mouth and held it there like a prize. She didn't take the bait at first, and waited, trying to make sense of the man in front of her. He was such an interesting mix, polite and respectful, and yet something behind his crisp shirt and tailored buttons seemed unpredictable and rebellious.

She'd had the tame before. This time, she wanted the wild.

Gabriella opened her mouth, allowing her lower lip to graze along his thumb before sinking her teeth into the cake, pulling it free from his fingers. His eyes blazed as she devoured it, like he was watching a show that wasn't quite suitable for public viewing.

Maybe Connor Starks wasn't going to be so boring after all.

THREE

Connor turned the hot water as high as it would go and let the scalding stream rush over him. It was a bizarre choice, since it was still over ninety degrees outside. He probably could have used an ice-cold shower after the way things had gone down this afternoon. But taking a hot shower in summer instead of a cold one was a practice his grandfather had taught him years ago. That way the air outside would seem much cooler when he was done.

His grandfather was full of good advice. Advice Connor needed. But he couldn't talk to his grandfather about what he really needed help with: how he'd ended up on a date with Gabriella Evans, and what the hell he was supposed do next.

He'd seen her before today. Actually, he'd noticed her the first moment she appeared by Jamie's side. It had been back in early June, when summer had just started to make itself known. She was beautiful—curvy in all the right places and strong in all the rest. He dug girls with glasses too. The sexy-smart thing always did him in, although those types of girls didn't have a tendency to run in the same circles he did. He didn't see her often, anyway.

She didn't show up at the beach parties he went to with Dean, and he'd been avoiding those kinds of nights lately anyway.

He kept wondering what her deal was every time he saw her on a street corner in town, or eating lunch by herself somewhere, but he never approached her, never asked Jamie to make the introductions or even find out her name. He'd made a point not to ask for it. She seemed untouchable somehow. Pure. Too perfect for him to mar. A girl like her needed to be taken out on expensive dates by a nice, well-mannered gentleman, and that sure as hell wasn't him. Besides, he was on a good streak now and needed to focus. He'd spent most of the last few months working, which was probably why Jamie had steamrolled him into going on a blind date. He said no right away, but then she'd gotten Dean on her side. Once they'd both started in on how long it had been and how he'd probably lost his touch, Connor begrudgingly gave in. He was only doing it to get them to back off, so he hadn't bothered to find out much about his date in advance. All he knew was that she was a grad student and only around for a few more weeks. That was fine with him. He'd never looked for anything more long term than that, so why start now?

But then he saw that *she* was the one waiting for him and everything changed.

He'd had a moment of panic, wondering why on earth Jamie had set him up with the first woman he'd ever been intimidated to approach. She seemed so sure of herself sitting in the café, so calm and detached, like an island. While Connor walked around his life with a kind of cocky self-confidence, he always felt a bit cracked open, like anyone could see what a mess he was inside if they looked hard enough. Her poise disarmed him. He couldn't call her Gabriella. The name, so formal it seemed almost royal, kept her firmly on the pedestal he'd put her on all summer. Calling her Gabby was the only way he could bring things back down to a level he could handle. The nickname seemed to suit her more, anyway, once she smiled and blushed.

He hadn't been prepared for how that blush would hit him, or the other million little things about her he hadn't caught from far away. How her blonde hair wasn't bleached and brittle, but was natural, a soft ashy color that fell down around her elbows. That her eyes were gray behind her glasses, unusual and striking. The hoop in her ear that suggested there was more to her than just a smart girl with a pretty face.

God, he was an ass for telling her she was pretty. What kind of idiot says something like that ten seconds into a date?

She *was* pretty, though. Not just pretty—gorgeous. Ridiculously gorgeous. In fact, she was so goddamn over-the-top sexy he could have killed Jamie for not warning him. She should have, should have warned him that listening to Gabby talk about numbers was going to somehow be the hottest thing he'd ever heard. That watching her bite the cake from his fingers would make him beyond thankful the table between them hid the hard-on he couldn't check. That stopping himself from turning on the charm when he walked her back to her car would be almost impossible.

It would have been so easy too. He'd pictured it happening as they paused in the parking lot: he'd talk his way into her passenger seat with practiced words. Give her directions to the secluded spots he knew so well he could have found them with his eyes closed, his hand up her skirt and mouth at her neck. Slip into the backseat and do what he'd done dozens of other times with dozens of other girls. But for some reason, he couldn't do that. Not this time.

Not with her.

The water started to run cooler, the heater having given him everything it could. Connor wanted to push it further, eek out just a few more minutes of seclusion in steam, but that would leave his grandmother with nothing to wash the dishes in, and he didn't feel like getting that particular lecture. Again.

He shut the shower off and the pipes groaned in gratitude. As he pulled back the curtain and scrubbed a towel over his skin, the cloud of humidity quickly escaped through the crack in the window. The mirror cleared, and Connor examined his reflection.

Once, he'd been scrawny as shit. At fifteen he'd barely cleared five foot. His voice hadn't lowered yet and there wasn't a prayer of stubble on his chin. His grandparents had been worried there was something wrong with him, even took him to a doctor to find out if he needed steroid injections or some crap, but then one day in tenth grade, he finally started growing. It was probably because he wasn't hungry all the time anymore and actually felt secure enough to sleep at night.

Now he had muscles. A growth spurt at sixteen followed by the job he'd needed to get had made sure of that. Heavy lifting and hard work were part of the deal. Dropping the towel, Connor lifted his chin and studied himself from all angles. Six-foot-four. Ripped arms. A six-pack that girls he'd been with had licked— actually fucking *licked*—but did Gabby see all that? Or did she only see the baby face he'd never quite grown out of and the way he'd quickly changed the subject when she asked about his degree?

There was no point in talking about his stint at Southern Maine Community College, chosen for its easy distance between home and work, while she was getting a freaking PhD. Who was he kidding? He didn't have a shot in hell with her. Not if she ever found out who he used to be.

"Connor, dinner's almost ready!"

His grandmother's voice filtered through the walls, a combination of sweet and don't-slack-or-there'll-be-hell-to-pay.

He knew better by now than to hide in the bathroom feeling sorry for himself when there was a table to set.

"Be right there."

He made his way into the dining room a few minutes later, dressed and dry except for a few last tendrils of hair. His grandfather raised an eyebrow from his chair at the head of the table.

"When I told you to take hot showers in the summer, I said take a shower. Not a monsoon."

Connor smiled and started setting out the napkins and plates piled up at his spot. "Sorry, Pops. I won't let it happen again."

But his grandfather wasn't done lecturing, and when Reginald Hapwood got on a soapbox about something, it was hard to get him off it.

"We taught you better than that. Twenty minutes is just a waste. And what's your grandmother going to wash the dishes with tonight? Water from the tea kettle?"

"Oh hush, Reggie."

Connor's grandmother came in from the kitchen, a pot roast in a white Corningware dish clutched between her oven mitt-covered hands.

"There's plenty of time for the heater to fill back up." She placed the dish on the trivet in the middle of the table, ignoring her husband's continued grumbling as she leaned over to kiss Connor's cheek. "How was your day?"

It was like something out of a fairy tale Connor had dreamed up during nights when his father hadn't come home yet, and his mother was strung out on the couch. A warm meal on the table. Clothes that didn't reek because they hadn't been washed. Haircuts when he needed them. Not having to stay home on school picture day because he couldn't afford to buy them. Family. Security. Love.

Sometimes he still had to remind himself that this was real life now.

"It was good." He waited to put his napkin in his lap until his grandmother sat down at the table. The second she was in her chair, his grandfather cut into the pot roast with vigor.

"Just good?" she asked with a smile that said she had a secret she wanted to share. "I heard you had a date with the Evans girl."

Of course she'd heard. Barbara Hapwood seemed to have a penchant for knowing everyone and everything, even though it also seemed she never left the house. His grandfather kept cutting with his eyes averted, but Connor could tell the old man was listening. It was in the slight pause of the knife against the meat. The way he made slower, nonchalant slices, far too interested in making the portion sizes equal.

Connor cleared his throat. "I did. We had coffee."

And cake. He couldn't forget the cake.

"Her grandmother was such a dear," she said, accepting the plate her husband handed her. "I was so sad to hear she'd passed. She had the loveliest rose garden. Is Gabriella staying at her house?"

Of course she knew that too.

"Yup, she is."

His grandfather didn't make eye contact as he handed Connor his plate. "She goes to that fancy engineering school down in Boston, right?"

"M.I.T."

"Hmm," he grunted.

What Connor heard, however, was, *Then why the hell is she interested in you?*

"So is she nice?" his grandmother asked. "What's she been doing up here, all summer long?"

"Yeah, she's nice." Connor was talking with his mouth full.

He didn't care. "And she's doing research. Some kind of math thing."

He was being purposely vague, not wanting to answer any more questions. He remembered, though—every word about the principle Gabby was trying to disprove. Duality. That it was mathematically impossible to replace something with its opposite.

He hoped to God that wasn't true.

"Sounds like you were listening real hard on that date," his grandfather remarked around a forkful of pot roast, his sarcasm louder than the sound of his chewing. He was punished for it with a teasing smack to the top of his hand by his wife.

"Don't give Connor a hard time," she scolded. "And both of you close your mouths when you eat."

When they were done and the table was cleared, Connor's grandfather retreated to the porch for the nightly cigar he was never allowed to smoke in the house. Connor lingered in the kitchen and offered to help with the dishes as hot water began coughing out of the faucet, but his grandmother shooed him away.

"Go join your grandfather. He seemed like he wanted to talk to you."

She turned to the sink and focused her attention on the dishes. Connor let his head fall back against the kitchen wall with a thud. He needed to talk to someone, but he wasn't sure his grandfather was the best choice. He didn't have very many options, though. His buddy Mikey wouldn't have a clue what to say, more from lack of experience than anything else, and Dean was practically useless when it came to giving good advice. What he needed was someone who had been there, someone who could tell him how the hell to turn himself overnight into the kind of guy Gabby would want to be with, even for a little while.

It made him wish his father was still around, for once.

Connor pushed off the wall and walked to the door. The humidity pressed in from the outside, still heavy despite the dwindling sunlight. He opened the screen and let it bang back against the building, announcing his entrance. But there was no greeting from his grandfather as Connor sank down into the Adirondack chair next to the porch swing.

For a long time they said absolutely nothing. Connor sat there and listened to the sounds of the coast getting ready for slumber—kids playing in the last gasps of twilight, the first chirps from the crickets, his grandmother humming along with the rush of the faucet. She shut the water off, following it with the gentle squeak of a towel against a plate. The porch swing creaked as Connor's grandfather rocked it back and forth. The air smelled of salt marsh and cigar.

"You working in the garage tonight?" his grandfather finally asked. It was the starter to a deeper conversation. A warm-up. The opening act.

"Not tonight." Connor would have, but then he'd probably need another shower. It wasn't worth the risk.

Another long moment of swinging and creaking passed.

"You like the Evans girl?"

Connor didn't know if he'd ever really *liked* a girl. Wanted, yes. Lusted after, chased, fucked standing up against the back of the lifeguard stand while a bonfire roared by the dunes—that was closer to the truth. And God, he wanted that with Gabby. Still, was that what made him hold back today? Because he liked her? Connor's face went suddenly hot, like he was that voice-cracking, scrawny kid again, and he'd just been busted for having a crush on the head cheerleader.

"Yeah," he said. "I like her."

His grandfather took a long, slow drag off his cigar.

"You know what I think?" It wasn't a question. "I think you need to clean up your act."

Connor pinched his lips together. Wasn't that what the past few years had been? Working himself to exhaustion while he tried to turn his life around?

"I thought I'd already done that."

"You know what I mean, Connor."

The familiar wave of anger swelled in his stomach. "You mean don't be like my father."

Through the open window, Connor heard his grandmother pause. The sudden absence of the sound of her towel squeaking against ceramic told him he'd hit a nerve. Regret seared through him, and he lowered his head like a puppy who'd just been admonished. Amazing how she could do that without even saying a word.

The squeaking started again, and his grandfather continued.

"That's not what I meant." The kindness in his tone made Connor feel even worse. One of these days, he was going to have to stop thinking everyone was against him. "I meant, with the girls."

Connor looked out past the porch railing. In the darkness, fireflies winked at him from the lawn. It wasn't that he didn't know his grandfather was aware of his not-so-savory past with girls. He just didn't *want* him to know about it. It was hard to avoid, though, considering how he'd behaved.

He picked at the hole in the knee of his jeans, the threads unraveling. "It's been a while since I acted like that."

"Hmm," his grandfather said again, bringing the cigar to his lips. This time, Connor knew exactly what that *hmm* meant. It meant he'd heard that before. It meant Connor had been so wild for so many years, breaking laws and breaking hearts, unable to be tamed after a childhood of lawlessness, it was hard to believe he'd come out of it changed.

"It's true. Besides, I don't want to be like that with her."

"Hmm." Another puff. "What makes her so special?"

Connor tugged on a loosening strand of frayed denim until it snapped.

"She's different," he said, knowing Gabby was a hell of a lot more than just that. She was the kind of girl who went beyond his wildest expectations. The kind he thought he could never have. "She makes me want to be different too."

"So be different."

Connor had no clue how to reply to that one. Wondering how to do exactly that was the reason he needed advice in the first place. But as the porch swing gently swayed, Connor finally figured it out.

Duality. Gabby's theory.

He could replace himself with his dual and become the opposite of who he once was. He could be a different version of the Connor Starks that everyone in town knew and pitied. A better version. A version Gabby would want to be with.

Then, maybe, he'd have a shot.

FOUR

"Are you going on another date with Connor?"

Gabriella looked up from where she was crouched by her grandmother's overgrown rose bushes. Jamie was on the other side of them in her own backyard, stretched out along a deck chair, her brown ringlets piled up in a messy bun on top of her head. She'd been lying there slathered in oil for hours while Gabriella attempted to garden, wearing a hat and covered in SPF-80. Jamie was a lifeguard and spent enough of her time outside that she didn't need to tan on her day off. Still, she'd been simmering in the sun for so long Gabriella was surprised she couldn't smell her friend's skin burning.

"Do you know that ninety percent of skin cancers are associated with exposure to ultraviolet radiation?" Gabriella asked.

"Do you know you're really good at not answering the questions I ask you?"

"Fine," she answered with a sigh. "Yes, I'm going out with Connor again. He asked me to go out for ice cream before we left the coffee shop on Saturday."

"Locking in the next date before the first one ends. That's good. I think he really likes you."

"Well, he was nothing but a perfect gentleman." Gabriella eyed the edge of the bush she was pruning. It had become wild without Nana's diligent attention, and she'd started the day with a pair of shears in hand, hoping she inherited her grandmother's green thumb. "He just walked me to my car after our date and didn't try anything at all."

"What were you hoping for? For him to attack you in your backseat?"

It was a rhetorical question, making it all the easier for Gabriella to say nothing. It was better Jamie didn't know she'd wanted something exactly like that. She'd been hungry for it after the Cake-Feeding Incident, and again after that when Connor lifted a leftover crumb from the corner of her mouth with his thumb. She wanted to lick it. She'd wanted to lick other things too.

"You thought he was cute, though, right?" Jamie asked, obviously not needing an answer. "I thought he was perfect for you, you both being geeks and all."

"I'm not a geek. I'm a mathematician. There's a difference." She snipped some bark away, freeing the last stem from its hardened casing. "But yes. I thought Connor was very—" She shook her head. Scrunched up her nose. "Cute."

Connor was more than just cute, with that perfect face and considerable frame, but their date turned out to be more frustrating than anything else. He walked her back to her car, and Gabriella had stared up at that God-forsaken little dip above his mouth, wanting to prove her theory that it was soft and supple. She needed to crane her neck to look at it. He was so tall that even with her almost on her toes she was barely eye-level with his shoulder. She was close enough, though, to tell him she enjoyed meeting him, that she'd be happy to join him for ice cream, and waited for him to take the first step. She wanted him to kiss her or at least give her another raised eyebrow or that glint in his eye again. Connor seemed momentarily torn, as if he were holding himself back from something. His eyebrows pushed together as he stared at her mouth, worry lines forming on his forehead. When he finally leaned in, all he did was give her a polite peck on the cheek, said he would meet her in town on Wednesday and walked away.

"I just don't think it's going anywhere," Gabriella said. "But I suppose I'll go out with him one more time."

The truth was that she couldn't figure Connor out, and nothing irritated her more than a problem she couldn't solve. His behavior walked the delicate tightrope between gentleman and bad boy, and she wanted to know why. Why he set her spine tingling with his eyes on her mouth at the café, and why he stopped right when he could have had more. She tossed her shears onto the grass and sat back on her heels. Connor was like a complicated proof she needed to take her time with, but after so much dissatisfaction and nights left wanting, patience wasn't a virtue she possessed anymore.

Jamie sighed and shook her head. "Your mom is right. You're never satisfied."

The words stung. Gabriella always thought that it was her mother, not her, who could never be satisfied. Despite all of her accomplishments, despite being accepted to M.I.T., passing her qualifying exams and having her thesis proposal accepted, the fact that she wasn't paired off to some loafer-wearing doctor-in-the-making somehow made her a failure. Her mother was still in the mindset that the pursuit of a man was more important than a career. It was another archaic conjecture Gabriella wanted to disprove.

"So when are you seeing him again?"

"Wednesday."

"Wednesday. Okay." Jamie sat up. "That gives us two days to figure out what you should wear."

Gabriella rolled her eyes. What was the point of putting any effort into figuring out what to wear if Connor wasn't going to put any effort into taking her clothes *off* her? She began gathering the roses she'd cut, bunching them together a little too quickly. A thorn scratched against her index finger. She winced and inspected the drop of crimson that beaded up on her skin.

"My clothes are fine," she insisted, her tone a little more forceful than she intended. Jamie didn't seem to notice.

"No, they're not. Maybe if you knew what to wear on a second date, you wouldn't be single."

"You're single."

"I'm not single. I'm weighing my options. There's a difference." Jamie stuck her tongue out. Then she shook her head again, more dramatically this time, as if to say how hopeless Gabriella was. "I'm going to make some margaritas. You want?"

"No thanks."

Jamie shrugged and went inside.

It was an unlikely friendship they'd formed the first summer Gabriella spent in Portland. She was nine and gangly and unsure of herself. Jamie, however, was always ready for a new friend and had knocked on Nana's front door within minutes of her arrival, asking if Gabriella could come out and play.

"Oh how wonderful," Gabriella's mother had trilled, practically shoving her out onto the front porch. "Someone to play with instead of doing math all the time."

Gabriella had been born with a knack for numbers, more at home with sums and products than other girls. She didn't get along with her classmates at the all-girls private school she attended, but Jamie had grown up with three older brothers and was happy to have a girlfriend around. Gabriella's mother had no idea what kind of influence Jamie was going to be that first summer. Despite the early awkwardness between them, their friendship grew to become something she secretly looked forward to every year. For the months of June through August, she deviated from the well-behaved little girl she'd always been. Instead, she ran through the sand dunes barefoot and learned how to play practical jokes, helping Jamie scare her brothers. The summer she was twelve, Jamie taught her how to apply lipstick and French braid her hair. Visits in her teen years were spent reading magazines that explained the "Rules of Dating," including how to kiss and when to let a boy go all the way.

That had happened for Jamie well before it did for Gabriella, her virginity lost midway through her senior year in high school. Jamie said he'd held her hand for hours first, that he'd been gentle, sweet and tender. Gabriella wasn't jealous—not exactly. She wasn't interested in slow and romantic. She wanted it hot and wet and dirty. She had no idea where those fantasies came from or why they were the spark that pushed her over the edge when her body ached in the quiet hours of the night, but she was desperate to know what that kind of raw, uninhibited passion felt like.

It wasn't until her freshman year at college that Gabriella was able to experience that. She hooked up with the R.A. of her dorm on Halloween. He'd been only moderately drunk, and she'd been ridiculously turned on by the way he pinned her down on his twin-sized bed, his fingers dipping into her panties and remarking huskily over the slick skin he found there. He was clumsy from the beer and not as easy on her as he would have been if he'd known she was a virgin, but she didn't offer the information. The sex was uncomfortable and disappointing in the end, but it was her first taste, a trial run, and each subsequent date became an opportunity to try for the grittiness she always wanted. Seven years and a string of boyfriends later, she decided the search was pointless. It also didn't mesh well with the other goals she'd nurtured for years: to become a well-respected mathematician and counter theories everyone else thought of as truth.

She lifted her head from the rose bush as a butterfly floated past her, its wings a wash of orange, yellow and black. She had to laugh at the coincidence. It had been when Gabriella stepped into the tattoo parlor in Cambridge and chosen a butterfly design for her ink that she realized that duality wasn't possible. The butterfly transformed from the ordinary caterpillar into something beautiful and wonderful, but that was a paradox that couldn't be physically reconciled in humanity. They were a dichotomy in nature, opposites but identical at the same time. It simply wasn't logical for a division of unity like that to exist. The tiny sunburst of color on her hip was a daily reminder of that.

Gabriella stood and rubbed the dirt off her legs. Creases lined her knees, echoes of the blades of grass that had been pressed against her skin for the last few hours. It felt good—evidence of the hard work she'd put in. Work she'd be willing to keep putting in if only her parents saw the value of this house. Here, where the doors were never locked and nature hummed quietly outside the windows, she was able to feel close to her grandmother again. It was a crime that her parents wanted to sell it. They'd only allowed Gabriella to spend the summer here until they found a suitable buyer. Despite all the pressure they put on her, despite the fact that they made her feel like she was never quite good enough, taking away this house was the only thing she truly hated them for.

She went inside with the handful of roses she'd clipped, took off her hat and filled a ceramic vase with water. Careful this time to avoid the barbs that protected the flowers, she dropped them into the vase and brought the arrangement into the dining room.

"Roses are a symbol of balance," Nana had told her years ago by the very rose bushes she'd just attempted to prune. "A rose represents promises and hope, but its beauty is bonded with thorns. It embodies pain and loss. Combined together, they are in perfect harmony, equal parts beautiful and strong."

She'd brought the lush rose petals to Gabriella's nose, letting her inhale the fragrance.

"You are beautiful and strong too, my darling Gabby. Always stay true to who you are."

Gabriella sighed and carefully arranged the vase on the sideboard across from the cherry oval table.

"Balance," she murmured, scrutinizing the delicate combination of petals and thorns. Maybe her grandmother's words could help her gather evidence for her thesis. She looked down at the finger she'd pricked and then ran it against the silky petal of a flower, testing its texture.

"If it's true that a rose is beautiful, it must also be true that the opposite is beautiful as well. A thorn may be the opposite of a rose, so therefore, is it also true that the thorn is as beautiful as the rose? No, it's not."

Gabriella pressed her thumb against a tiny sharp spike and smiled triumphantly at her supporting conclusion. Her grin slid into a frown, though, as she continued to chafe the pad of her thumb with the thorn. Was the pain she felt when it grazed her flesh any less pleasurable than the smooth touch of the flower? Were they truly opposites, these two sensations she craved? Or were they merely two sides of the same coin? If a thorn wasn't as beautiful as the rose, how could she lust for the roughness of a firm grip as much as she hungered for the sweet bliss of shattering pleasure?

Gabriella released the rose and turned to study herself in the mirror above her grandmother's ornate sideboard. She traced a still-wet finger along the glass.

"A mirror image is the dual of its original. Water molecules must be arranged as H_2O in order for them to act like water. Theoretical Mathematics says that Oxygen-Hydrogen-Oxygen and Hydrogen-Oxygen-Oxygen are the same, but in the real world, those molecules aren't water. In fact, they don't even exist. Therefore duality can't apply to mirror images and must be incorrect."

It was a sound hypothesis. But if her mirror image wasn't her dual, then the woman staring back at her wasn't the same as Gabriella. She certainly felt like two fractured parts, two pieces of the same whole scattering in opposite directions. If her rider appeared at that moment and wanted to tie her to the bed, wanted to take her out in the backyard and fuck her senseless where everyone could hear, would the part of her that calculated and planned enjoy it as much as the part of her that ached for the raw slap of a spanking?

As if on cue, she heard the sharp buzz of tires ripping around the corner.

Gabriella moved to the window to watch him ride past. He was covered in head-to-toe leather, denim and steel, as always. He must have been melting under all that clothing. Once again, she imagined stripping his jacket and gloves from him, revealing sweaty skin and rippled muscles. The strong body that would take her as brutally as she'd always wanted.

He slowed and her heart stopped, as if her fantasy was actually coming to life. But he drove on and she pinched her eyes shut, feeling like an idiot for the way hope had leapt up her throat. Wanting her rider was ridiculous. She was water lusting after oil, a coupling that would never mix. That's why Jamie had set her up with Connor, after all, and not with someone like *him*.

She had to let the fantasy go. She wouldn't let it exist anymore.

Turning from the window, Gabriella searched the room for more evidence to disprove her theory. She found nothing.

"I'm getting nowhere," she said. "And I'm talking to myself again."

FIVE

When Gabriella returned to the Old Port for her second date with Connor, the sky was beginning to turn pink, lines of gold and yellow streaking across it as the sun dipped down below the watery horizon. It was still warm out, and the town was filled with people. She had to circle the parking lot several times before she found a space.

A breeze kissed the skin on her thighs as she got out of her car, and she flattened her palms against her sides to stop her skirt from flaring up in the air. The billowy yellow skirt, white blouse and flowery sandals she was wearing had actually gotten Jamie's seal of approval, but Gabriella didn't see the point. Connor was probably going to be a perfect gentleman again.

She walked across the brick and cobbled stones, ten minutes ahead of schedule, as usual. Even though the date was probably going to be a waste of time, that wasn't a reason for her not to be punctual, right? Besides, being early would mean she could get a spot in line before Connor got there and maybe get this whole ordeal over with as quickly as possible.

She arrived at the ice cream parlor only to freeze mid-step.

Connor was already there, sitting on top of a picnic table outside the shop's front door.

"You're early," she announced.

He launched off the tabletop and smiled at her the same way he did at the café—the smile she'd been hoping for when he left her at her car. His mouth curled up and his eyebrow seemed to follow it, as if the two were linked. It was a grin of a hungry cat seeking a mouse, and she wanted to be chased and found.

"I didn't have far to walk. My office is only a few blocks away. And besides—" Connor moved in close to her, closer than she anticipated, and brushed her hair off her shoulder. "I was looking forward to seeing you."

His closeness surprised her, but she relished the opportunity to study him. His hair was a little more unruly today than the last time she saw him. The shorter strands by his forehead fell forward, brushing past eyes that were sparkling in the waning sunlight. A black, short-sleeved shirt outlined his chest and arms. Somehow, he was so much sexier than she remembered.

His gaze trailed down her frame, devouring her as if she were the piece of cake this time. Her body started to heat, her breath picking up under the intensity of his stare, but then his smile morphed into what looked like doubt. He dropped his hand and threw an awkward glance toward his shoes, the moment between them fading before Gabriella had a chance to savor it.

He waved a hand toward the ice cream parlor. "Should we get in line?"

Gabriella nodded and took a few steps toward the crowded entryway. It was a popular spot for tourists and locals alike, and she stopped at the end of a line so long it drifted out the door.

"How was your day?" she asked. "More coding of stuff?"

Connor chuckled. "Pretty much. I stare at screens all day long. It's like *The Matrix* in there."

"And all you see is 'blonde, brunette, redhead,' right?" she asked as she turned to grin at him, quoting the film.

"No," he said. "Just blonde."

Gabriella blinked, then realized he was talking about her. Her lips twitched and she fought the urge to smile, blushing intensely as she turned back around to face the doorway. Connor bounced from flirtatious to serious and back again so quickly, it really confused the hell out of her. Especially when his sweet little compliments strummed a romantic chord inside her she didn't think she had.

They inched through the doorway, their bodies nearly jammed together as they edged slowly toward the counter. She felt Connor's breath on her neck, sensed the broad expanse of his chest against her shoulder blades. The line moved up, and his large, warm palm met the small of her back, urging her forward. His touch was like an electric shock to her system. She lifted her gaze to meet his, wondering if he felt it too, but he quickly averted his eyes and nodded at the case of flavors on display.

"What are you gonna have?"

She went up on her tiptoes, canvassing the options. "I think I'm going with the salted caramel today. Can't go wrong with a mix of savory and sweet." She glanced back to him. "You?"

"I always go with vanilla. Boring I guess, but I like it," he said. "Are you the kind of girl who likes a cup or a cone?"

"Oh, a cone for sure. You can't eat a cup. I want the most bang for my buck."

He chuckled. "A very logical answer."

Gabriella grinned wide. "Of course."

She ordered two scoops in a cone while Connor got the largest cup they had. When they reached the register, he once again refused to allow her to pay. She tried to argue with him, but he playfully nudged her away.

Gabriella looked around at the tables in the parlor. They were all full. "Doesn't look like there's anywhere to sit."

"It's a nice evening for a walk." Connor angled his head toward the door. "Shall we?"

Yup, he was going to be all-gentleman tonight. She plastered a smile on her face and followed him to the door. He held it open for her, and they set out along the streets.

"Do you miss Boston much?" he asked. "This place must be pretty boring for you after growing up in a big city."

"Actually, I really like it here. Don't you?"

Connor shrugged and stared into his cup. "I guess it's not the same when you've lived in the sticks all your life."

"I wouldn't call it the sticks."

Gabriella sighed happily and looked around at the old, red brick buildings set in footprints of stone. The alley they were walking through was alive with music and the soft clink of silverware against plates. Old-fashioned streetlamps dotted each corner with perfect precision. The evening air smelled of pine trees and low tide—cool, clean and calm.

"I love the charm here," she said. "The sea and the mountains surrounding the city. It's so peaceful."

"Right. Nature girl." He grinned at her, and it made her grin back just as wide.

"Well, there are some really good trails, but I also have happy memories of being here. I was free from my parents' expectations for a little while. It was my escape."

She surprised herself at her honesty with him once again, but there was something about the tempering presence of the ocean and the lulling sound of Connor's voice that drew back the walls she kept so tightly around herself.

"Your folks were pretty hard on you?" Connor scooped up another big mouthful of ice cream, and Gabriella tried not to focus on the way his tongue lagged over the edge of the plastic spoon.

"Were?" she asked with a snort. "They still are." She almost added that their constant distance and propensity to judge were slowly killing her, but she forced the thought away, not wanting her baggage to become a third wheel on the date. "But I guess all parents hard on their kids, right?"

"I wouldn't know. Mine took off years ago."

Gabriella stopped walking. "They took off?"

Connor paused as well and frowned at the ground.

"My dad left when I was thirteen. Apparently, his next fix was more important than we were. I found out he died a few years later."

He looked up, squinted and pinched his lips together, as if the words had a bad taste to them. "Mom tried to manage for a while, but she was using too. She couldn't make ends meet, so she left me with my grandparents when I was fifteen to go into rehab."

"Wow. How did that go over?"

"Weird at first, since I'd never met them before, but they took me in right away, no questions asked. Of course that was because Mom said it would only be until she got out of rehab."

"She didn't go?"

"She did. She just never came back."

Gabriella's mouth fell open. For all her parents made her crazy, she couldn't imagine being abandoned like that. "I'm so sorry."

Connor shook his head and let out an abrupt laugh. "Don't be. She made the right choice. She couldn't have handled me anymore. I was a real rebel back then. I needed some serious discipline."

Something inside her flared at the word rebel, but she squashed it down.

"So your grandparents raised you?"

"Yup. They made me clean up my act. Taught me to respect others and to play by the rules."

Gabriella's stomach bobbed like a buoy on the tide. She wondered exactly how dirty his act had been and what rules he'd forgotten to play by, but she concentrated on her ice cream instead as they resumed their stroll down the street.

"My grandmother always taught me to just be myself," she said. "Even when my parents seemed to want the exact opposite."

"They don't want you to be a mathematical genius?" He smiled at her, and that damn dip under his nose taunted her again.

"They do, but my mother wants me to find a safe, rich husband and settle down too."

"And that's not what you want?"

She halted on the corner and looked up at him. There were so many things she wanted, the least of which was the comfortable parameters of the kinds of relationships she'd known. No, she wanted Connor, wanted those brawny hands of his pushing her up against a wall and showing her all about the rebel he once was.

She flattened her tongue against the shaft of her ice cream and licked. Slowly.

"No. That's not what I want."

Connor's breath rushed out on a tight exhale. He stared hard at her, his towering body looming, leaning in close. Gabriella's belly tightened in anticipation of his lips finally brushing against hers, but then someone on the street called out his name. They jumped apart as two male voices hollered loudly from the cab of a pickup as it sped by.

"Friends of yours?" she asked.

Connor watched the truck, his body tense and guarded until it was out of sight. Then he let out a slow, deep breath.

"Yeah. Sorry about that. Some people never change, you know?"

She didn't know. She'd never had anyone yell out of a truck at her, never stared at one as it disappeared from sight the way Connor had, either. He cleared his throat and nodded in the opposite direction from where the pickup had gone.

"So how's your research going?" he asked, making it clear that talking about whoever had just passed by was off the table. She wished he'd let her in, because having another piece of the mystery that was Connor unsolved was almost as frustrating as how damn good he looked in his jeans from behind.

Gabriella followed him away from the lights of the streets and toward the dimly lit wharf. "Pretty badly, actually. I'm having trouble gathering evidence, which will make it interesting when I meet my thesis advisor in the fall and I have absolutely nothing to show him."

"Well, disproving duality can't be easy. I mean, everything is dual to some extent, right? Everything's opposite is also its equal. North and South. Good and evil." He grinned at her, lips quirking up again, eyes crinkling. "Autobots and Decepticons."

Gabriella laughed loudly. It felt good to abandon their former heaviness.

"That's the proof I need. I can base my entire thesis statement off *The Transformers*." She waved her hand dramatically in front of her. "I can see the title now: 'Eighties Cartoons Invalidate Central Theory in Projective Geometry and Boolean Algebra'."

"It could work."

Connor wolfed down the last spoonful of his dessert and tossed the bowl in the trash before they drifted in the direction of the docks. When they came to a point where a gate locked the pier, a *No Trespassing* sign guarding it, Gabriella stopped.

"Dead end," she noted, but Connor typed a code into a

keypad by the knob, and the catch in the metal door released. He opened it for her, and Gabriella eyed the pier down at the end of the ramp. Sailboats and yachts floated and rocked in every slip. "Do you have a boat down there?"

"No, but like I said—I know my way around codes."

"And I'm guessing *No Trespassing* signs don't apply to rebels like you, either."

He laughed and held her gaze. "Something like that."

His voice was soft and low, his eyes hooded and dangerous again. The Connor she'd seen for a few moments at the café was back, and she wanted more of him. She stepped through the open gate and waited as he closed it behind them. The ramp was steep, and they walked down the length of ropes and wood to the flat of the dock. It was steady, secured in place by tall poles made of timber, moss growing where the water broke around them. The noise from town quieted and was replaced by the softly lapping shore, the creak and groan of idling boats, and the sound of their footsteps. As they neared the edge of the pier, Gabriella was intensely aware of Connor's presence and the fact that in between the moored boats and sleeping seagulls, they were completely alone.

"I still don't see how you can disprove duality," he continued. "Every extreme is a variation of its dual, right? Hot and cold are opposites, but really, they're just degrees of the same thing."

Gabriella enjoyed his logic, even if he wasn't understanding the whole picture. "So you're saying that light and dark aren't opposites. They're just two poles of the same phenomena."

"Exactly."

"Good theorizing. I'm impressed." She leaned back against one of the poles and slicked her tongue over the pool of melted ice cream in her cone. "Do you have any other examples to share with me?"

"Tons." Connor braced an arm above her head, his body so

muscled and sure and towering over hers. "Love and hate. Repulsion and attraction."

She felt the pull between them like magnets. Like gravity. She had to know if he felt it too.

"Pleasure and pain."

"Exactly," he repeated softly. "I mean, how can you try to disprove something when it's standing right there in front of you?"

She licked her ice cream again. Connor's eyes darkened as his gaze dipped down to her mouth, his heavy stare fixed on her tongue. Gabriella broke off a piece of the sugary cone and bit down on it sharply. She heard his breath catch.

"Going for the cone already when you haven't finished your ice cream?" he asked.

"I guess I've had enough." The truth was that she was nowhere close to full, her body empty and throbbing with the need to be taken and claimed.

"Well, I finished mine, and I'm still hungry." His mouth was inches away from hers. "Sharing is caring."

She tilted her half-eaten cone toward his mouth. Connor leaned in, his eyes locked with hers as he slipped his tongue inside it. He probed and licked, achingly slow, his tongue sliding into the wafer funnel the way she imagined it pushing into her body. She shivered and reached back to clutch at the wood behind her with one hand, her knees starting to buckle.

"You sure you don't want any more?" he asked.

"I might want more." But she didn't mean the ice cream.

"You should. It tastes really good."

He took the cone from her hand and slowly, purposefully gathered some ice cream onto the tip of his tongue. Closing the distance between them, he bent down to brush his lips against hers. For a moment, all she felt was hot breath and cold lips, and then his kiss washed over her. Gabriella melted into the feeling, drinking the ice cream that spilled from his mouth into hers.

Connor pulled back to take a breath and threw the cone to the ground.

"You taste better." He roughly clasped her neck, cleaving her to him for another dizzying kiss. "Goddamn, you taste so good."

Everything that had been pent up inside her suddenly released. Gabriella returned his kiss in a frenzy of want, not caring how the move dug her glasses into her face. He leaned in and that wall of muscle lining his abs just barely grazed her nipples. Wanting him closer, she reached forward and grasped the belt loops of his jeans, trying to yank him toward her.

"No," he whispered harshly. "Hands behind you. Leave them there."

She choked out a strangled moan. The dirty taunt and command in his words was something she'd wanted to hear for so long, something she'd been desperate for. Obeying, she moved her arms behind her until she felt the rough support of the pole again, and Connor kissed her, hard. His hands tangled in her hair, pulling and twisting and arching her up for more. She gasped at the sensation, a sound that Connor swallowed until he broke the kiss to smile wickedly at her.

"That feel good?" he asked, tugging the rope of hair he'd coiled at her nape. She could only nod, too much of a panting, needy mess to reply. He chuckled and bit at the side her mouth. The decadent pinch made her buck against him. "Fuck, you're so sexy."

Pleasure spiraled through her, meshing with the abrasion of the wood on her back and hands. Connor pushed her against it, his body pressing, tongue seeking, teeth rasping. He freed her hair and raked his hands down her sides, then moved to her waist, his fingers sinking into her flesh. It pushed him more firmly between her legs, and Gabriella whimpered when she felt the thick outline of his erection through his jeans.

Connor hiked up her skirt and she flexed her hips, an involuntary move, her mind lost to instinct. His hands found her ass and tilted her hips up toward his thrust, giving him ample space to slide his denim-covered cock along the damp cotton of her panties. Her clit swelled and throbbed, soft and warm against hard and unyielding. He dipped his tongue into her mouth, and she wanted to slide her fingers into his jeans in the same way. She wanted to disobey his order to keep her hands behind her, to shimmy her back down that pole until her knees met the uneven slats of the dock and take that hard length of his into her mouth.

So she decided on doing exactly that.

Her hands shook as she lunged for his jeans, her fingers snapping to the buttons and pulling them free. She'd just run her palm over the cotton underneath, feeling the dampness where it touched his thick, blunt head when Connor hissed and stopped her. With a grunt, he pulled her hands up to his mouth. He kissed her knuckles, his lips lingering there, the move almost reverent as he gently pressed his forehead against hers.

"Fuck, Gabby. You..." He trailed off, his breathing coarse and jagged. "You are not what I expected."

Gabriella closed her eyes. "Neither are you."

SIX

Connor slammed the gate shut and thundered back down the dock. He didn't stop walking until he was at the water's edge, as far as he could get from the parking lot where he'd said goodnight to Gabby and then took off.

What the fuck was the matter with him? Was he actually going to try to be different this time around, or was all that just bullshit to get his grandfather off his case?

He plunked down on the edge of the dock and hung his legs over the water. It was dark, the sea black and deep, and he felt so stupid he almost wanted to hurl himself into it. Still, he didn't know how the hell he was supposed to have resisted Gabby tonight. She was unreal, quoting *The Matrix* and *Transformers*, turning his inner geek into a drooling idiot, all while licking her ice cream like she was giving head. How on earth had she made something so innocent look so goddamn hot? It was like watching porn, for Christ's sake.

Connor closed his eyes and brought his hands up to his face, hoping that grinding his palms against his eyelids would force the picture of her mouth from his brain. But as images of what else he wanted to slide past those soft lips of hers began to fly through his head, he reopened his eyes and let his hands fall back to his lap.

He hadn't planned on bringing her here, hadn't consciously realized he was leading her to this secluded spot where few would find them. He'd broken the code to that lock at the gate years ago, after watching enough snooty yacht-owners try to deftly hide the keypad with no idea how easily they were giving the numbers away. He'd just planned on meeting Gabby for ice cream and then maybe taking a nice walk around town. Nothing *else* was going to happen. They were going to be in public after all, although that had never really stopped him before. Then the opportunity presented itself, and he couldn't resist.

Connor lifted his hands to his face again and cupped them around his mouth, sucking back a few shallow breaths. He hadn't counted on her being as tempting as she was—as eager and sexy and more responsive than he'd ever imagined. As soon as she unbuttoned his jeans and touched him, he almost lost it. He had to stop things when he did, had to walk her back to her car and keep a healthy distance between them, making up some bullshit about being parked in another lot and bolting away like he'd just thrown a Molotov cocktail in her backseat. If he hadn't, he would have been leading her into the belly of some shoddily locked yacht, and he'd be playing out the same pattern all over again.

He couldn't let that happen. No matter how frisky she was getting on the docks, Connor was sure she wouldn't go as far as he would. She'd never want to see just how bad he could be.

Damn it, if he didn't act differently around her, how was he going to convince her he was worth her time?

He winced and shook his head. He'd done more than wish his father was around—he'd started to turn into him. Shit. All these years he'd hoped not to be anything like him, and here he was, putting up a front for Gabby that wasn't so different from the crap his old man fed his mom.

Patricia Hapwood had been raised with a good head on her shoulders, had a diploma under her belt and plans to make something of herself. But when Travis Starks rolled into town with a vintage Harley for wheels and a cross hanging from one ear, all her good sense went out the window. It was the eighties, and Travis was a dead ringer for Rob Lowe in that eighties movie *St. Elmo's Fire*.

That's what Patricia always said, anyway. Travis told her he was going to take her on an adventure, that he was going to be the best thing that ever happened to her, and she believed him. She snuck out in the middle of the night and he rode her out of Portland, took her down Route One from the rocky coastline of Maine to the palm trees of Southern Florida, getting her hooked on crystal meth along the way. They got married somewhere in the Keys and were making their way back north when Patricia found out she was pregnant. She wanted to raise a kid in Maine so they set up camp in Augusta, and she stopped using until Connor was born. Money was tight, even tighter when she got hooked again. The adventure Travis promised her turned into renting a shitty apartment and working the morning shift as a cashier at Cumberland Farms. Patricia never bothered to tell her parents she was back, even though they were only living fifty miles away. As a matter of fact, until Connor was fifteen, he never knew his grandparents existed at all.

The familiar buzz of a motorcycle barreling down Commercial made Connor snap to attention. It was the sound that once heralded Travis's arrival home. His father loved the shiny beast he rode, took better care of it than he did his own family. Occasionally when a gear or filter on it needed fixing, Travis would call Connor out to the asphalt to help. He'd listen to instructions, making sure to hand over the right tools, learning everything he could, wanting to show his father that he was worthy of his attention. Travis would even take him out on it once in a while, and those times sitting between his father and the open road were the only happy memories of him that Connor had.

There weren't a lot of them.

Most of the time Travis came home late, tired and covered in grease and in a hurry to light up. Odd jobs in dirty garages didn't put food on the table, not when you had a habit to support. Patricia's job didn't help much, either, although it did mean she was at least physically present when Connor got off the bus, even if she was too high to help him with homework or make something that resembled dinner.

Connor wrapped his arms around his stomach. Even all these years later, he still remembered exactly what it was like to go to bed hungry and wake up even hungrier, how the need for food had turned into nausea by the time he broke into his first store.

He'd been twelve when he did it—just the local deli when there was nothing left in the house to eat. The cops caught him, carted him back home and threatened his parents with words like court and Child Protective Services, but it ended up being a total joke. They didn't change, so Connor kept stealing, and the cops kept reeling him in. It wasn't until Travis ran out of patience with the responsibilities of being a husband and a father, riding out of town for good, that Patricia tried to sober up enough to be a parent.

That, apparently, had been another joke.

The bike in the distance picked up in speed until the sound of it vanished, and Connor inhaled a shaky breath. Because of his father, Connor knew engines inside and out, knew the difference between a single, a V-twin or a boxer just by hearing its growl. He could figure out what was wrong with a bike simply by the vibration of its handlebars, knew just how to make a machine roar to life and then calm into a patient, powerful idle. Until he learned his way around computers, working with motorcycles was all he could do. And even after that, it was the only way he could make any money. It was how he paid his way through SMCC. But Connor didn't want that life anymore. Grease on his fingers wasn't the way to a better future, to a life that didn't look like his father's.

A life that included a girl like Gabby.

What he'd told her about his first months in Portland had only been the tip of the iceberg. He was a mess when he got here, even more so when he realized his mother wasn't coming back. He started tenth grade at South Portland High angry and defiant and eager for a fight. Word about who he was and where he came from spread fast, but at the time, Connor didn't care about the bad rep. He mouthed off to his teachers and wore his detention slips like badges of honor. He got a tattoo just for the hell of it, got into fights with the football players and had their cheerleader girlfriends whimpering out orgasms behind the bleachers. One night his senior year when he got tired of walking into town for parties, he stole his grandfather's car. Only after he was pulled over and brought back to their house in cuffs did he discover what being grounded was like.

It wasn't fair to treat them like that when they'd done nothing but support him, but Connor guessed that when you grow up without any limits, you're constantly trying to find out what finally crosses the line. There was no way in hell he wanted Gabby knowing about all that.

Connor drew his legs up to his chest and hugged his knees. After that night, his grandparents told him he was on his own if he didn't get his act together. That as soon as he turned eighteen, he was out. The idea of losing the only family he had left in the world terrified him, and he'd done his best to cut the crap. He started studying, started getting better grades and avoiding brushes with the law. He got into SMCC and spent his days working at the shop and his nights going to class. He stayed on there after he got his degree, building up his skill with bikes while reading books on coding and making a couple of low-budget websites on the side. He managed to leave most of his rebel past behind him, but it wasn't as easy to change his habits with girls as it had been with everything else.

While drugs and empty promises may have been Travis's way of luring a woman in, seduction was Connor's. Somehow he'd figured out the right way to smile, learned how to talk softly and look at them in a way that would make their pupils dilate and their nipples hard. He knew what to whisper in their ears, words just dirty enough that they would follow him anywhere. They'd hide in the dark with him and gasp in surprise at the lewd things he liked to do, crying out that no one had ever made them feel so good or come so hard.

And that's where it always ended. After the last panted breath was where Connor cut things off. He'd never asked a single one for her phone number. He had no desire to spill his soul, to tell his whole sorry story and see the pity in their faces. He didn't want to become someone's project or to try to make sex turn into something more. He had no clue how to be in a relationship. How could he, considering his parents' shitty example? But being with Gabby made him want to figure it out.

It was a shock to realize just how much he wanted her around and not just for a little while. Opening up to her came easy. There was no judgment in the way she looked at him with those big, gray eyes. No, he saw a familiar kind of pain there, something he recognized but couldn't quite put his finger on. He wanted to *know* her, to have a chance to be with her, not just have a fling that lasted until summer was up. His only hope of success was hanging on whether or not he could pull off being the Connor he was trying to channel, the one that didn't have a reputation with the authorities. The Connor that built computer programs instead of engines and didn't try to get into his date's pants up against a pier. If he kept acting on his impulses, he was going to lose her. But how the hell was he going to avoid that when she kept tempting out the parts of him he was doing everything possible to rein in?

There was no way he was going to survive this.

Taking a deep breath, Connor heaved himself up off the dock and took his ass home.

* * *

"Hey, Starks—what's the E.T.A. on finishing that shopping cart?"

Connor looked up from his screen. Lines of code were stretched across it. The same lines he'd been staring at for the last hour. His boss, Mark, hovered above the partition that separated Connor's desk from the rest of the office, waiting for a reply.

Connor cleared his throat. "Almost done. I'll upload it to the test server before noon."

It was Independence Day, and they were closing up shop early. He only had an hour left before everyone took off. He should have been done this morning, but he kept getting distracted.

Mark tossed an apple into the air. They were Linux users, yet Mark brought the shiny fruit to work almost every day, eating it as he went through their invoices, as if the act in itself was a rebellion. It was part of why Connor fit in here—they were their own sort of dissenters, promoting universal access and redistribution of a product's source code as opposed to the proprietary software that the giant companies like Apple used.

Mark caught the apple and grinned. "Good deal."

Connor ducked his head and refocused on his work. There was no excuse for him being this late on a project, but he'd been thinking about Gabby nonstop since the night before, despite resorting to his hand and some lube when he got home. And again in the shower this morning.

His mind was in a constant loop, remembering how she'd responded to him, the way she'd whimpered in surrender when he barked out a command, and then the look in her eyes when she tried to unbutton his jeans. He couldn't get a read on her. Was Gabby the kind of girl who would want to be in charge, or would she wait for him to take the lead? What kinds of noises would she make once he got her somewhere private and stripped off her clothes and glasses?

God, those glasses. He'd hoped she'd take them off, curious to know what she looked like without them, but they'd remained prim and proper on her nose and that had made everything they did seem even naughtier.

Would she want to keep them on while they did it too?

Fuck, that would be hot.

Connor closed his eyes and sucked back a grunt. He had to stop thinking like that. Damn it, this was why he hadn't gotten a fucking thing done all morning. He couldn't remember the last time he'd been this messed up over a girl.

Redoubling his efforts, he stared at his screen again. If he could just concentrate, he could finish this shit in a half hour. It wasn't hard—for some reason coding came easy to him.

It had been Dean's dad who wanted a website for his auto body business a few years back. Figuring it couldn't be too difficult, Connor had parked himself in front of Dean's computer and threw something together after a couple of hours of research. The day the site went live, Dean's dad got seven more jobs alone. Mikey's dad was next, wanting more clients for his landscaping company than he could reach within the confines of local advertising. A month after Connor built that site, their client base tripled. Since then, they'd expanded as far north as Yarmouth and far enough south to have some jobs along the New Hampshire border.

Connor's grandparents had seen promise there and encouraged him to enroll in the Computer Science program at SMCC, if he could work enough to pay his way through. By the time he started his classes, he realized he knew more than most of his professors. He never thought he'd actually be able to build a career on it, but he liked the way it challenged his thinking. And it always amazed him what he could do with a computer, what he could build with nothing more than a keyboard and his brain. Everything else in life cost too much money for any hope of achievement. In programming, all you needed was a seven-dollar-a-month hosting account and some ingenuity.

Getting this job had been a total crapshoot. Mark and his team had come up from New York City and put together a start-up in an old warehouse overlooking the wharf. They weren't picky with resumes, didn't care about experience or what history the Starks name held. They just threw Connor a coding test when he showed up for his interview and asked him to figure out the bug. It had taken him five minutes. They hired him on the spot.

Connor tapped out a few more lines, hit a snag and sat back to think, rocking in the plush leather chair at his desk. It wasn't his, really. Everything in the wide, open space of the office belonged to Mark, but Connor had earned his spot here. A small collection of personal items filled his workspace. On the hutch sat a tiny Hot Wheels yellow-and-black Camaro, a miniature version of the Transformer, Bumblebee. A framed photo of him with his grandparents was next to his screen, and his favorite Buddhist quote was tacked to his corkboard:

Make an island of yourself, make yourself your refuge. There is no other refuge. Make truth your island. Make truth your refuge.

It always made Connor think about how he was on his own in

this world. How after being abandoned by the people who were supposed to love him unconditionally, the only truth was in his ability to rely on himself.

A sudden flash of inspiration hit, and Connor sat forward, unfurling several lines of code. He smoke tested it, and once he was sure it was working, uploaded it to the staging server and logged off.

"We're good," he informed Mark as he stood. "I'm out."

Mark flashed him a wave, and Connor pushed through the door, taking the steps two at a time until he hit the pavement. It was a perfectly clear day—the kind that didn't have a trace of humidity, summer's heat forced into temporary submission by a cool sea breeze. Was this the kind of weather Gabby went hiking in? And would she ever be willing to take him with her? He could give it a try, although he'd never gone into the woods for any reason other than to find a tree wide enough to hide a girl behind or to escape from the cops.

The former would be much more preferable to do with Gabby than the latter.

The smell of fried fish wafted across the street and Connor's stomach grumbled. Lobster rolls and chowder were what made the seacoast famous, and Gabby's words about Portland the night before had made him appreciate this town in a way he hadn't before. He crossed Commercial, stopping at the corner sandwich shop, and was just digging into his lunch when his cell phone rang. He snapped it off his belt loop and checked the screen. The last person in the world he wanted to talk to at that moment was his grandfather. The second to last person was currently calling.

Connor picked up the call. "What, Dean?"

"You hitting the fireworks with us tonight or what?" Dean had the call on speaker. Connor could hear the sound of wind blowing and country music in the background—a sure sign that he was driving the pickup and Mikey was riding shotgun. "And who was that girl you were with last night? Someone you found on a dating site for the hottest female nerds in New England?"

"Funny. And thanks for the drive-by right before I was about to make a move, by the way. You two really know how to help a guy out."

"Glad to be of service," Dean replied. "Mikey, will you at least turn that shit down?"

Connor waited until the sound of southern twang faded. "Don't you guys ever work?"

"One of the perks of being employed by our fathers. Slacking comes with the territory. Besides, it's the Fourth of July. The day's over, my friend."

It was true. And soon everyone in a ten-mile radius would find themselves a small square of real estate in Bug Light Park. He'd put money on the fact that Gabby and Jamie were going to be there too.

"There a reason why you're not answering me?" Dean asked, pulling Connor back to the here and now.

"Because I'm eating my lunch," he lied. "And because you're a jackass."

That part was the truth.

He swallowed a bite of his sandwich and gave in. "Yes, I'll be there tonight. And I was with Gabby Evans last night. The girl Jamie set me up with."

"Hold up." Connor heard the sound of a fist pounding the dash, and the radio went silent. "You went out with the same girl twice?"

"Since when do you know so much about my dating life?"

"Since when do you go on actual dates?"

Connor sighed. Dean was right, but he didn't feel like explaining everything. "I like her, okay? I want to get to know her."

"Well, fuck me."

"That's what she said," Mikey added with a laugh. Connor ignored him.

"You'll have to introduce us to her tonight at the park," Dean said. "See you at nine."

Connor ended the call without saying anything else. Goodbyes weren't necessary with Dean—the first friend he'd made when he came to Portland, a partner in crime found in the back row of detention. Having Dean and Gabby in the same place wasn't a combination Connor was looking forward to. If he was lucky, there'd be too many people there for that to happen at all.

He didn't exactly have a history of being lucky.

Still, as he looked around at the sunny wharf and thought of Gabby's smile, it seemed possible that his luck might finally be coming around.

SEVEN

Gabriella locked her grandmother's front door and threw her keys into her bag. Locking the door felt odd—she didn't have a single memory of her grandmother ever carrying a key. But the house was her responsibility for the summer, and she couldn't bear the thought of anyone breaking in. She wished she had the money to buy it herself. Losing this place was going to be like losing Nana all over again.

Jamie stood at the end of their driveways with her hands on her hips.

"Red, white and blue? Really?"

Gabriella looked down at her clothes. "It's the Fourth of July. What's wrong with it?"

Jamie threw her hands in the air and started walking. "I don't know how you could have grown up in Boston and still have zero fashion sense."

"You know I don't care about that."

She didn't. She definitely hadn't chosen the red tank because it clung to her breasts in just the right way, hadn't picked out the blue-and-white striped shorts because she knew they made her ass look good. This outfit wasn't for Connor and the hope that seeing her in it would push him over the edge. It would be a nice surprise, though.

She'd hoped he would have asked her to go with him to the fireworks after their date, but instead, all he'd done after rebuttoning his pants and righting her wrinkled skirt was walk her back to the parking lot, gave her another well-mannered kiss on her cheek and left her at her car. Fueled by confusion and frustration, she'd given in to fantasies about her rider when she got home, thinking about all the things she was sure he would have done to her on that deserted pier. The way he would have watched her sink to her knees, the feel of the thick, heavy ridge of his cock pushing against her tongue. His touch as he spread her out on the dock and slipped his hand into her panties. Alone in her bed, Gabriella rubbed her needy, swollen flesh until her rider's phantom fingers made her shudder into her pillow. But the solo session left her feeling empty and frustrated.

She didn't understand Connor's advances and pauses, pulling back just when she wished he'd give her more. There was something hidden in his eyes when he talked about his past, about the reckless teen he once was, but maybe she was imagining more than was really there. Connor couldn't be both the rebel and the geek, couldn't be the bad boy turned good. Duality like that might be found in nature, but she'd had enough experience to know that it didn't exist in men.

Gabriella followed behind Jamie as she led the way to Bug Light Park. The sidewalks were already crowded with people carrying lawn chairs and towels to the green by the shore. It was where the town gathered for the fireworks on Independence Day, and it was a tradition Gabriella had loved every summer she'd been there. They reached the edge of the park and stopped where a bottleneck of people had gathered, trying to find space on the quickly filling lawn. While they waited for a break in the traffic ahead of them, Gabriella came up on her toes and scanned the crowd.

She wasn't looking for dark hair and a lumberjack build. She wasn't.

"Looking for Connor?" Jamie's smile proved there was no point in trying to lie.

She did anyway.

"No. I was just seeing where there might be some spots to sit." Gabriella straightened her spine, defiant. "I don't know why you're pushing this so hard."

Jamie crossed her arms. "Because he's perfect for you. Trust me."

She was about to ask why when she heard the sound of a motorcycle's rumble. She turned in the direction of the low, idling growl with just enough time catch to the smirk on Jamie's face before it vanished.

"You *do* know him, don't you?"

"Who?"

"The guy on the bike."

"Which guy?" Jamie pretended so well at the picture of innocence, Gabriella was surprised a halo didn't materialize above her head.

"You know which one."

"So what if I do? I thought you only liked dorky guys."

"Maybe I wanted a change."

Jamie grinned merrily. "Oh, Gabriella. I know you better than you think I do."

She wanted to ask her friend about her cryptic response, but then they were interrupted by a tall, rugged-looking blond who pulled Jamie into a one-armed hug. The hand that was pressing her to him boldly clutched an open bottle of beer.

"Jamie Matthews, my favorite girl."

"Oh, I'm your favorite now, huh? You'd better let all the other girls know." She swatted his chest and pushed him away. "Dean, this is my friend from Boston, Gabriella."

"The famous Gabriella!" A grin washed over his face as he looked her up and down. "I've heard a lot about you."

"Oh yeah? What's Jamie said about me?"

"Not from Jamie. From my boy, Connor. You're the girl he won't shut up about."

"And you can stop talking right about now."

Gabriella whirled around at the sound of Connor's voice, catching sight of him as he cut through the crowd. He came to her side and gave Dean a threatening look, but it didn't seem to affect him at all.

"Sorry, buddy. I speak the truth," Dean replied. "She might as well know what a sappy fucker you are before she gets in deeper."

"Thanks, man." Connor sighed and dug his hands into his pockets, quite possibly to stop himself from strangling Dean, who saluted Connor with his bottle.

"No problem. Mikey's got a cooler up at the tent. You ladies want to join us?"

"I'm up for a free beer," Jamie cheered, immediately hopping on Dean's back. He let out a whoop and carried her up the hill, leaving Connor and Gabriella alone.

"Hey," he said.

"Hey." *Kiss me again.* "I was hoping to see you here tonight."

"Me too." He kicked at the grass and nodded in the direction of the sea of tents in front of them. "Do you want to get a beer? I mean, you don't have to drink. We've probably got some water too, if you want that."

He was babbling. It was adorable.

"You think math students don't drink beer?" she asked. "The motto at M.I.T. is 'work hard, but play harder'. Well, that, and 'sleep is for the weak'. It means we spend half our time guzzling caffeine and the other half getting wasted."

The grin that spread over Connor's face made Gabriella realize she was babbling too. She, on the other hand, felt somewhat less than adorable. She lowered her head, trying to hide her face in her hair.

"What I mean is, yes, I'd love a beer."

Connor chuckled. "Good," he said, leaning his shoulder down toward hers. "You look really cute tonight, by the way. The red, white and blue, I mean."

Gabriella beamed. "Thank you."

He led the way, finding a path through the colorful towels that formed a blanket over the lush grass. The sun had already begun to set, and people were whistling at the moored boat on the horizon that housed the fireworks. They stopped at a worn tent being guarded by a wiry kid with black hair and glasses too big for his face.

"Connor's here," he said. "Now the party can finally start."

"This is Mikey," Jamie explained to Gabriella as they all sat down in front of the tent. "Also from South Portland High."

She reached over and shook Mikey's hand. Connor sat down next to her and stretched out his long legs in front of him until they brushed against hers. Gabriella shifted an inch closer so they were touching.

"These three go way back," Jamie added.

"*Way* back." Mikey pulled a bottle from the cooler and handed one to Gabriella, offering one to Connor next. He shook his head. "Dean was famous for the most detentions in the ninth grade, but Connor busted that record when he showed up in tenth." Mikey looked up at him admiringly. "This guy really knew how to party."

"Mikey—"

"Hey, remember the Fourth the summer we got our

licenses?" he asked, apparently ignoring the warning in Connor's voice. "When we tore donuts with Dean's truck into Sheriff Roger's lawn?"

"Yeah, I remember," Connor said. "And I was so glad that I was the one who got caught for it while the two of you were already home."

Dean tilted back his bottle for a long sip. "Good times."

Gabriella could feel the muscles in Connor's leg tense. It was obvious he didn't want this story told, but her curiosity was piqued. She couldn't help wanting to hear more about his rebellious past.

"Why did Connor get caught for it when it was Dean's truck?" she asked.

"Well, Sheriff Roger already kind of had it in for him," Mikey continued. "He was the one who'd practically knocked up his daughter after all—"

"O-*kay!*" Connor said loudly as he sat up straight, his body going taut like a switchblade. "I think we don't need to go there tonight."

Gabriella shouldn't have wanted to hear the last part of that story. There was nothing about him being so reckless with someone else that should have turned her on, but it just reminded her of the night before and how willing Connor was to press her against that pole where anyone could see.

Exactly what else had he done? And why wasn't he willing to do it with her?

"Oh I think we definitely need to go there, my friend," Dean argued, sliding an arm across Gabriella's shoulders. Connor's jaw ticked, eyes flaring at where Dean's skin touched hers. "Don't you think our girl here deserves to know everything about the guy she's into?"

Connor's lips pinched together as he looked away. Whatever

his friends were teasing him about was a layer he didn't want peeled back right now.

"I think I know a lot about Connor already," Gabriella said. "And I think there's a lot more to him than you all know too."

Connor smiled at the ground. It made all her joints go a little bit loose.

"Oooh," Dean catcalled, releasing Gabriella from his grip. "You sure you want to know *everything*, Miss Ivy League?"

There was a dare in his words that flustered her, but it got cut off when Jamie suddenly stood up.

"Hey, you know what? I think the fireworks are about to start." She started walking backwards toward the water. "I'm going to get a closer spot. Anyone coming?"

Dean looked after her, paused for a moment and then leapt to his feet. "Sounds like an invitation to me."

He started chasing Jamie down the hill. Connor shot a glare at Mikey, who quickly stood too.

"Um, I'll go get the other six pack from Dean's truck," he muttered before hurrying away.

Gabriella nursed her beer as the group scattered. The sky had darkened to a deep purple, and a sea breeze rushed in with the incoming tide. It made her hair fly about her face, and she rubbed her hands over her arms, trying to chase away the gooseflesh that rose from the chilly air. How unlike her to have forgotten to bring a sweatshirt.

"You cold?" Connor asked. "We can watch the fireworks from inside the tent if you want?"

"Sure. That'd be nice."

He stood and helped her up. His hand felt warm and big as his fingers wrapped around hers. They ducked their heads inside the tent, and when they were sitting back down next to one another, Connor unzipped his sweatshirt and draped it over her shoulders. The fabric was warm. It smelled like him—a clean, woodsy scent laced with a hint of sweat.

She breathed in and threaded her arms through the sleeves. "Thank you." Connor nodded and tied back a tent flap so they could still see the sky, then drew his legs up and rested his elbows on his knees. Despite his size, he looked like a little boy, lost and unsure.

"You okay?"

He made a sound that was a little too painful to be a laugh. He shook his head, his gaze falling down between his bent arms. "I'm fine. I'm really sorry about Dean and Mikey. They really are good guys. Most of the time."

"They weren't so bad." She gave him what she hoped was a reassuring smile and carefully added, "I like getting to hear more about you."

"You say that now." Connor took a breath and looked up. He didn't face her, though. Just kept his eyes trained on the ocean's edge. "That wasn't the worst of it. I told you I wasn't a good kid."

"You were young. Besides, good isn't always what it's cracked up to be. It's boring and entirely too overrated."

Connor smiled over his shoulder at her. With his mouth pressed against his bicep, she could only see his grin in the way his cheeks lifted, his eyes crinkling at the corners. It made her heart leap in funny ways. Then his stare turned heavy, gaze dropping and lingering at the edge of her top. His eyes grew hooded, the look in them suddenly dangerous again, and Gabriella teased her fingers along the neckline of her tank in a silent suggestion. She wanted more of the Connor who kissed her on the dock, the rebel who trespassed and slept with local officials' daughters. It went against everything she should have wanted, everything she'd come here to prove, but she didn't care.

Connor lifted his head and balanced his chin on his arm.

"You don't like being good, Gabby?" His voice was hushed, his words a slowly igniting flame.

She shook her head. "There's a lot more to *me* than you know too."

"Yeah?" He shifted around and planted one hand on either side of her hips, caging her between them. "You want to be bad?"

She nodded slowly. Without a word, Connor took her beer from her hand and set it by the edge of the tent. He carefully slipped her glasses from her face, placing them to the side. He looked her over and smiled, then reached up to her ponytail and slid the elastic free. There was something intensely erotic in the feeling of that tight circle gliding out of her hair. Gabriella closed her eyes as he feathered his fingers through the loose strands. She could have purred at his soft touch, but then he made a fist at the base of her skull, and she gasped, her eyes flying open. The pull against her scalp felt too good, a sharp pleasure-pain that made her teeth sink into her lip. Connor smirked and curled her hair even tighter into his grip, pulling her down until she was lying on her back.

"Bad girl," he whispered.

The fireworks began, the first loud explosion of light and sound echoing above them as Connor licked into her mouth, his tongue probing and seeking. He released her hair and gathered her wrists together, raising them up over her head while his other hand traveled down to the curve of her breast. He stroked over the stiff peak of her nipple, moving on top of her as he pinched and tweaked. The sensation sent off a spark that went straight between her legs. Gabriella's hips bucked up against his at the stab of pleasure, settling him further into the cradle of her thighs.

"More," she pleaded. "Please."

"God, Gabby." Connor began grinding against her, finding a rhythm that pressed his fly into her shorts, a delectable chafe that made her moan. "You make me want to be so fucking bad with you."

"Do it. Show me how bad you can be."

He kissed her deeper, teeth tugging at her lower lip as he let go of her wrists. She drove her fingers into his silky hair, and he rolled them to their sides, breaking the kiss to push his sweatshirt off her shoulders and fumble with her top. He couldn't seem to stop himself from kissing her in between his desperate grappling with her shirt, ravenous kisses that stole her ability to breathe properly. Her tank was halfway up her torso when Mikey suddenly popped his head into the tent.

"I got the beers—"

Connor twisted up angrily off Gabriella, his body shielding hers. Mikey froze.

"Oh. Dude. Sorry."

He dropped the six-pack in the corner of the tent and quickly backed out. Once he was out of sight, Connor dropped his head and inhaled slowly, several times. Gabriella tried to do the same, her logical side knowing she had to even when her body screamed for more.

"Gotta calm down," he said. "Shit, Gabby. It's really hard to behave myself around you."

"I don't want you to behave."

He laughed and when he looked away, her heart faltered. For a moment, she could see the same look on his face that she'd seen so many times before, the same words in his expression: *You're too much of a freak for me, Gabriella Evans.* She waited for him to say it, to turn her down, to make her feel like there was something wrong with her, but instead, Connor simply smiled.

"Okay then. Maybe I won't."

EIGHT

This had to have been the dumbest decision Connor ever made. Either that or he had a death wish. He wanted Gabby so bad it was killing him. Still, if he was going to croak, watching the last of the fireworks go off overhead with her curled up between his knees was a pretty damn nice way to go.

After Mikey's interruption, Gabby had put her glasses back on and crawled into his lap, breathing in a soft sigh of contentment as she drew his hands together over her belly. With her back to his chest, she drank her beer and he held her close, his weight shifted so the top of his left arm was hidden from view. Without his hoodie on, the sleeves of the shirt he was wearing didn't quite hide the ink around his bicep. He didn't know what she'd think of it, despite what she said about good being overrated. Besides, it was a symbol of his life in a different time, and it was another part of his rebellious past that he was trying to keep solidly behind him.

The final burst of color lit up the sky—rings of blue with red crackling around it, all of it ending in a waterfall of white that left glittering tracks in its wake. Everyone clapped and cheered, and

Connor kept his arms tightly around Gabby as the crowd began to gather itself up, hundreds of feet about to make their way back out of the park. He pressed his lips behind her ear again and breathed in deep. She smelled of the ocean and summer and freedom.

"I always loved the Fourth," she told him, her words nearly lost under the sound of so many voices, of engines starting and folding beach chairs. "It was my favorite time of year."

"Are you a big fan of fireworks in general? Or just especially fond of the perils of our forefathers?" He nipped her earlobe and she wriggled in his grasp. "I bet you have the entire Declaration of Independence memorized."

"Shut up." She twisted away from his assault on her ear and then settled back down. "I loved it because it came at the beginning of summer vacation. I had lots of time left before I had to go back home."

Connor felt something sharp burrow its way into his chest. He wasn't sure if it was because of the sadness in Gabby's tone or the reminder that in a few weeks' time she was going to leave him.

The wind picked up and he pulled her closer. There were so many questions he wanted to ask. What was the deal with her parents? And why the hell was she here all by herself? Hadn't any of the guys she went to school with figured out how amazing she was?

"Jamie, Dean and Mikey are coming back," she said.

Gabby put her empty bottle by the edge of the cooler, and Connor reluctantly withdrew his arms from the warm space underneath hers. She stood up and brushed her legs off, giving him a spectacular view of her ass. He groaned and rubbed the flats of his palms over his forehead, counting to ten and thinking of dissecting frogs, of Red Sox stats—anything other than the view in front of him—before standing up behind her. Dean and Jamie trudged toward them, Mikey in tow.

"So what's next?" Dean asked as he flung an arm over Jamie's shoulders.

Dean was like that, the kind of guy who saw bare skin and wanted to touch it, never caring who that skin belonged to. Jamie didn't seem to mind, but Dean was a dead man if he ever touched Gabby again. The memory of his arm draped casually over her shoulders made Connor's stomach churn. He was going to make sure they had a talk about that later.

"Next?" Gabby glanced over her shoulder at Connor and then at Dean again. "There's a next?"

"Sure. The night is young," he replied, lowering a hand, no doubt, to slip into Jamie's back pocket. "I'd say let's chill here, but we finished all the beers in the cooler, and I don't think Mikey got to drop the second six pack in."

He said the last bit with a wink at Gabby. She pinched her lips together and glanced up at Connor with an embarrassed smile, her cheeks now adorably rosy from her beer. He smiled back at her. Mikey avoided eye contact with both of them.

"How about the tavern by SMCC?" Dean suggested.

Connor tensed. Mikey raised a hand and called out, "Shotgun."

"We're walking, douchebag," Dean replied, shoving him to the side. "There's five of us. We won't all fit. Or are you gonna make the ladies sit in the flatbed?"

Mikey frowned. "Gabriella can ride with Connor."

Gabby hooked her bag over her shoulder, head cocked to the side as she threw a quizzical gaze in Connor's direction. "You guys didn't come together?"

Dean's eyes flickered to his.

"Oh we did," Dean answered quickly. "But I really don't feel like driving through that huge mess of people. And—" he added with a satisfied grin, "—I'm drunk."

Jamie's giggle masked the sound of Connor's sigh. The tavern wasn't a bad spot. Just a local joint he'd been to more times than he cared to count. People who knew him might be there, people who knew the old him and didn't have quite so much discretion as Dean, although that wasn't saying much. Connor didn't like the idea of taking Gabby there, but then again, he didn't like the idea of having to say goodnight to her yet, either.

He held out his hand. "I'm in, but since you just made that announcement, hand over your keys. You're not driving until you sober up."

"Since when did you become the responsible one?" Dean reached into his pocket with his free hand anyway, fished out his keys and slapped them into Connor's palm.

They packed up the tent and the cooler, dropped the contents in the back of Dean's truck and then walked until they reached the campus edge. A line was leading into the bar, a bouncer checking IDs at the door. Connor watched Gabby bend over to fish her wallet from her bag. The move made the back of his sweatshirt ride up, once again showing off her ass in those tiny little shorts. It wasn't fair, the way she made a scrap of blue and white cotton into the sexiest thing he'd ever seen.

He stepped in close behind her in the line. "I like you in my sweatshirt," he whispered in her ear.

She turned so her cheek brushed over his mouth. "I like wearing it."

Connor slid his hands around her hips. Everything about his stance said *mine*. He'd never cared about anyone enough to want to stake his claim this way. The change felt good.

They moved in a pack toward the door, flashing their IDs before going inside. The tavern was crowded, music playing loudly and a line three people deep at the bar. Connor glanced around. No one he knew was there. He exhaled in relief.

"It's been a while since I let Dean beat me in pool," Jamie said. She took Dean's hand, leading him toward the back of the bar. "Come on, you. Let's wait for a table to open up."

Mikey glanced uncomfortably back at Connor and Gabby.

"I call winners," he said, hurrying after them.

A high-top by the window was open, and Connor gestured toward it. Gabby nodded, her eyes bright. He liked her this way—smiling and relaxed, like she'd unwound a part of herself and let him in. He wanted to be let in, wanted answers to the questions he'd had about her all summer. Maybe now, while they were in a place where he'd be forced to behave, was his chance to find out.

They hopped up onto the chairs, and Connor said, "All right, now that you've heard about my past, I think it's my turn to get to know more about you."

Gabby seemed to consider this. "Fair enough. But I don't think I've heard nearly enough about you yet. How about a deal: a question for a question?"

Just like at the café, Connor was unprepared for the way she got inside him, how she edged herself under his skin in a way no other girl ever had. He was beginning to think he'd let her ask him anything.

He held a hand across the table for her to shake. "Deal."

She shook it, business-like, and then her expression dissolved into a broad grin.

"You first," she said. "What do you want to know?"

He'd start off easy. "When did you get into hiking?"

The sparkle in her eyes softened a little. "It was something I did with my grandmother. We'd go on these nature walks and she'd tell me all about flowers and plants. It was really different from my life at home, the vigorous schedule, the expectations and school."

Her eyes went glassy. Connor wanted to reach across the table and touch her cheek, comfort her somehow.

"You must really miss her."

She nodded. It was a brisk movement, one that begged for him to change the subject.

"Will you take me hiking with you?" he asked.

She found her footing then and gave him a sly smile. "Now, now, Mr. Starks. That's two questions in a row. That wasn't part of our deal. But yes. I will."

"When?"

"You aren't very good at sticking to your agreements, are you?"

"I never said I was." He wasn't backing down until he got another date out of her. "When?"

She crossed her arms. She was smiling, though. "Saturday."

"Saturday it is." He put an elbow on the table and rested his chin in his hand. It was just an excuse to move closer to her. "Your turn."

She leaned in and balanced her crossed arms onto the table too. It gave him another spectacular view, this time of her breasts. It was torture to drag his eyes up to her face.

"Why'd you do the sheriff's daughter?" she asked.

Connor coughed out a laugh. It wasn't a question he expected her to ask. But he wasn't about to tell her how he'd fucked the sheriff's not-so-innocent little girl in the backseat of daddy's cruiser after she'd lifted the keys from his uniform pocket. How she'd pleaded with Connor to do it again when he didn't have a second condom, and how after the near-miss that followed, he'd made it a habit to carry more than one on him. He could indulge Gabby, though, and let her hear a little bit about just how bad he once was.

"Because it was wrong and I could," he answered.

Gabby narrowed her eyes. "You answered that really quickly."

He shrugged, enjoying the way she was looking at him. She wasn't horrified at all.

"It's the truth."

"Still, that was too fast. It barely even counted as an answer. I think I'm due another question."

He laughed again, harder this time. "Fine. A freebie, but only this once."

Her smile grew wide, her chin lifting in victory.

"How does a guy who tore donuts into the town sheriff's lawn turn into a computer geek?"

"You're really stuck on that, aren't you? I wasn't even the one driving."

Gabby leaned in closer. The view got even better. It was nearly impossible for him to keep his eyes on hers.

"I'm waiting," she said.

He made a face and let out a dramatic sigh. "Fine. It's a boring story, actually. Dean liked to cause trouble, and I liked to cause it with him. But we had to grow up eventually, and for whatever reason, coding was something I was good at."

It was almost entirely the truth.

"And you taught yourself everything you know."

"Pretty much. I read a lot about it, practiced on a few small-budget sites. I never had any classes in it before college, other than high school typing."

She seemed satisfied with that, so Connor took the opportunity to move on.

"My turn. Why did you get into math? I mean, what was the appeal?"

Gabby paused for a moment, as if she was weighing the worth of his question.

"It's clean. Ordered. There's no emotion involved. The answers are definite. Logical."

He could understand that. Emotions were definitely something he'd attempted to avoid.

"Coding is like that too. It either works or it doesn't. There are no gray areas to deal with."

"Right, completely the opposite of my grandmother's rose bushes, which seem to be dying on me no matter how many articles about gardening I read."

They smiled at each other for a minute. Connor had managed to keep his gaze north of her chin and now found himself stuck on how perfectly clear her skin was, how it seemed to glow. On her heart-shaped face and the way her cheeks lifted when she smiled. Things he'd never noticed about any girl before, ever.

He cleared his throat and rapped his knuckles against the table. "Um, it's your turn."

"Right." She looked up at the ceiling in thought, then back at him. "Most embarrassing moment."

"When my grandmother wanted to use my laptop to look something up and my browser was still open to a porn site."

She buried her face in her hands. "Oh my God, that's awful."

He had to laugh along with her. "It was."

She uncovered her eyes, her still hands shielding either side of her face. "You shouldn't bother asking me the same question. Yours wins, completely."

"Nah, that wasn't what I wanted to ask," he said. "Why are you here all by yourself?"

That seemed to rattle her. Her hands slid down from her face to the table. She picked at her napkin. "I told you, my parents and I don't really get along."

"I didn't mean them. I meant, why are you single? Are all the guys at M.I.T. blind?"

Gabby opened her mouth like she was on the edge of replying and blinked several times. She eventually smiled, but her eyes didn't light up the same way they usually did. It didn't match.

"I've had some short relationships, if you could even call them that. But none of them really...worked out." She spaced her words apart in a way that made Connor sense he'd touched a nerve.

"Same for me," he said, hoping it would get rid of the tension at the table. The little V between her eyebrows disappeared, and she wagged a finger at him. He wanted to bite it.

"I didn't ask about your relationships," she said. "That doesn't count as one of my questions."

"But you wanted to know, didn't you?" He knew she did, and strangely enough, he wanted to tell her. "Okay. Have at it. What's your next question?"

She leaned an inch closer. "Do you miss your parents?"

"No."

"Wow. Another quick answer."

"It was an easy question."

"Gotcha." She didn't push the subject, much to his relief, but instead lifted a hand to cover a yawn. "Sorry, I'm a little tired. I'm usually up at dawn, and I think that beer just got to me."

"You want to head out?" he asked, trying his best not to look disappointed. "I can take you home."

"Oh you don't have to do that. It's not a far walk."

"No way. It's late and it's dark." He didn't want her walking all the way back alone.

"Well, Jamie is probably ready to go too." She glanced at the pool table. They'd started a game, and Jamie was laughing, an open palm pressed against Dean's chest. She wasn't going anywhere anytime soon. At least, not with Gabby.

Connor hopped off the chair and pulled the truck keys from his pocket.

"If I know Dean, he won't let Jamie go until he's let her win at least twice. Besides, they're all trapped here until I say so. I'm the designated driver, remember?"

She slid off her chair too and looked up at him.

Say yes.

Give me a little more time with you.

"Okay. Just let me tell Jamie that you're taking me home."

He watched as she found her way to the pool table and cupped her hand around Jamie's ear. Dean was leaning low, about to take his shot, but then looked up and met Connor's eyes across the room. Connor dangled the keys to the truck in his hand, pointed a finger at Gabby and tilted his head in the direction of the door. Dean gave him a silent nod. If nothing else, at least almost a decade of friendship had made him into a halfway decent wingman.

Gabby hurried back, and this time, she was the one to take Connor's hand in hers when they were out on the street again. He didn't let go of her until they got to Dean's truck.

"Connor?" she said when he fit the key in the ignition. He paused and looked across the bench seat. She was curled up in his sweatshirt, hair messed up from the windy sea air and looking so fuckable he could hardly stand it. "I had a nice time tonight."

Whether she was talking about the fireworks or the tent or the bar, he had no idea. It didn't matter.

"Me too."

She smiled and blushed. When he pulled up in front of her house, she didn't rush to get out of the cab. Connor cut the engine.

"One more question," he said.

Her eyes were wide. Serious. "Yes?"

He swallowed. Of all the things he'd done, what he was about to ask somehow seemed the most daunting.

"Can I have your phone number?"

Gabby laughed loudly at that. It was possibly the most beautiful sound he'd ever heard.

"Of course. I'll give you my email too." She dug into her bag and pulled out her phone. "Give me yours. We'll trade."

Connor handed his phone over and took hers in return. He held it for a minute, enjoying touching something that belonged to her. When they'd given each others' phones back, Gabby seemed to hesitate for a moment, then slid slowly across the bench until she was right next to him.

"I have one last question too."

He could feel her breath on his face. "You want to keep my sweatshirt."

She grinned and shook her head. Then she pulled off her glasses, folded them closed and put them on the dashboard. His dick twitched in his pants, just like it had when he took them off her in the tent. She rocked that whole sexy librarian look, big time.

"Can I get a goodnight kiss?"

"A goodnight kiss," he repeated. She nodded. "I think that would be all right."

"Good."

She leaned in and brushed her lips shyly over his. It was gentle at first, and he let her control the kiss, let her choose the pace and the pressure, slow and soft. But then she changed the game on him, opening her mouth and sliding her tongue along his. She made the tiniest noise of pleasure when she did it too, and Connor couldn't stifle his groan. He slid his right hand around her and settled it into the dip at the small of her back, pulling her forward until she had no choice but to press herself against him. She rose up on her knees to put her hands on his shoulders, and Connor gripped the steering wheel tightly in his left hand. It was the only thing keeping him from grabbing her hips, tearing off those tiny cotton shorts of hers and pulling her down on top of him.

It seemed to last forever, until his hands got sweaty and the windows began steaming up around them. Gabby sucked his lower lip into her mouth, then giggled and wrapped her arms around his neck.

"We're gonna get in trouble if we keep this up," she said.

"I have no problem with that."

He didn't bother to say that he was pretty sure he was in trouble already.

Gabby shimmied away and put her glasses back on. She turned back to grin at him, one bare shoulder peeping out of his sweatshirt and her hair falling over her face. She looked like his wildest schoolgirl fantasy come to life. She needed to get inside before he cracked.

She wriggled out of his sweatshirt and handed it to him. "Goodnight."

"Night. See you Saturday."

She hopped down out of the truck and closed the door. Connor watched her cross the lawn, resisting the urge to lift his sweatshirt to his face and breathe in the scent she was sure to have left behind on it until she was out of sight. When she finally went inside, he buried his nose in the cotton. It smelled amazing.

He dropped it into his lap, mashed his head against the headrest and stared up at the ceiling. God, he deserved a fucking medal for holding himself back like that. She was hitting all his trigger points, finding everything that set him off and making him harder than he'd been in his life. He didn't just like doing it in public—it wasn't just the thrill of getting caught. He got off on being totally filthy with a girl, in watching her completely give in to lust regardless of where they were. That wasn't happening with Gabby in the cab of Dean's truck, especially after their little question and answer period that had only made him like her more.

Connor sighed and started the engine. He hadn't found out everything he'd wanted to, but they had time. He'd be seeing her in two days. He could ask her more questions on the hike.

If he was able to keep his hands off her, that was.

With a smile that stretched his cheeks to cartoon-like proportions, he drove back to the tavern. It had cleared out a little since they'd left, and he snagged a spot out front. He found Dean in the back, still at the pool table. Mikey was playing him now and losing. Badly.

"Where'd Jamie go?"

Dean sank a solid then stood up. "She's about to ply me with some coffee. Just went off to the bartender to ask them to brew me a pot. What is it with these women trying to make honest men out of us?"

"You're sober enough to drive, then?"

"I will be soon."

"Good." Connor handed over the keys to the truck. "Thanks for letting me take Gabby home. By the way, if you ever touch her again, I'll kill you."

"About that." Dean balanced his cue against the table. "You're into her. I can tell. But you might want to back off on this one."

Connor's smile hit a pothole. "Why?"

"Because she is who she is, and you are..." Dean waved a hand in front of him. "You."

"What the fuck is that supposed to mean?"

"Whoa, chill. All I mean is, she seems like kind of girl who might take certain *things* seriously."

"Things...like, sex?" Connor chuckled. Dean didn't know the half of it. "Don't worry about it. We're good on that front."

"So you've changed your M.O. with her, then?"

"Well, no—"

"Ah. I'm guessing she wasn't the one who started up shit with you back in the tent, right?" Dean nodded back over his shoulder. "I think poor Mikey's been scarred for life."

Connor's fingers tingled with the familiar need to curl into fists. "She was into it. Trust me."

But it made him think. Which one of them had initiated things in the tent, or even the other day on the docks? If he thought about it, the reality was, both times it had been him. And Gabby's kiss in the truck had taken things at about a quarter of the ridiculously fast pace he'd been careening towards whenever he was around her. Still, she hadn't so much as flinched when she'd heard a few more details about the reckless kid he'd been. She said she saw more in him, and that made him want to show her everything.

Dean bumped a fist against his shoulder. "All I'm saying is, she doesn't seem like your type. And you probably shouldn't get involved anyway. She's outta here in a few weeks. Not the best time for you to get all emo over a girl."

It was a little late for that.

And she *was* leaving but not yet. He still had time to get this right.

NINE

On Saturday morning, Gabriella didn't jump out of bed as usual, ready to start the day. She just lay there, staring at the ceiling. She'd been awake half the night, her pulse pounding in anticipation, too excited to sleep. In a few hours, she'd be spending the day with Connor—an entire day away from her research and her doubts, filled instead with clean mountain air and him by her side.

As if she'd have been able to get any work done anyway. She was supposed to have spent Friday working, but her thesis prep remained untouched, especially after getting an email from Connor confirming their plans for today. She hadn't been able to think about anything but him since he dropped her off two days ago.

She turned her head to glare at where her laptop sat folded up on her desk, shadows crossing over the cover. Outside her window, wind chased the early morning sunlight through the tree limbs. The sight made her sigh. The angle of the sun was already a little bit different than it had been when she first got here in early June. Although this part of the summer once held so much promise for her, today it was a reminder of how the clock was ticking. She was running out of time before the fall semester began, but it was impossible for her to concentrate on that now.

She still hadn't quite recovered from what Connor did to her in the tent at the park or the way he kissed her in Dean's truck. How he'd gripped her with that one big hand and pulled her to him, every line in his body stretched tight as a wire. Gabriella closed her eyes at the memory. Even when she'd been so sure what they had wasn't going anywhere, he'd proved her wrong. This thing between them was another paradox: him the unstoppable force and her, the immovable object. A duality, and both could not be true at once. If an irresistible power existed, then it logically followed that that there couldn't be any such thing as an unyielding entity, so how much longer could she deny what she craved? With Connor, she'd finally found a glimpse of what she'd been looking for, even though locking up that side of her was the thing she came to Portland to square away. She thought she had to prove to herself she couldn't be both sides of the coin, that she had to pick one way to be, that there was no way to be both. All her logic was failing her.

"If A equals B, then if you do the same thing to A and to B, the results will be equal," she said to the empty room. "I am 'A': an intelligent, independent woman, a mathematician who wants a successful career."

But if that was true, then could she be the same woman who was willing—no, *eager*—to let Connor grind against her in public, with no shame about who might catch them? She couldn't, and yet, she was. She was both A and B, two halves of the same, and both wanted Connor to fuck her senseless.

She threw off her blankets and reached for her bathrobe, the air in her bedroom chilly despite the calendar. She'd always loved the twin natures of the seashore in the summer: the way the midday sun would bear down until the insides of her knees and elbows were soaked with sweat, but then needing to pull a sweatshirt from her closet once the sky went purple with twilight. Maine summers could be two things at once, so why couldn't she?

When she was freshly showered, her hair twisted up in two French braids, she dug through her closet to find her hiking boots, thick socks and sturdy shorts. The sports bra and Henley tee she gathered into her hands would have appalled Jamie, but a hike was a hike whether it was a date or not, and Gabriella was always prepared.

She giggled at the thought and wondered if she should bring a condom too.

With her backpack in hand, she went outside to wait on the porch. For a moment, the vision of her rider taking her on it flashed through her mind. But she was too excited to see Connor to be distracted by silly fantasies. She searched through her bag for the trail map of Bradbury Mountain State Park. She was still studying it when the gate creaked open and slammed shut.

Gabriella looked up, startled. Connor was standing on her lawn, and her heart hammered at the sight of him. He'd made no attempt to discipline his hair today, and the dark locks fell about his face, tossed by the steady breeze. His grin was lazy, hands thrown into his shorts pockets as he wandered up her path. The tight sleeves of a blue Superman T-shirt gripped the magnificent muscles on his arms. She almost forgot how to talk, how to do anything but stare, and she was pretty sure by the way he stopped and smirked at her from the walkway that he could tell.

She remembered how to make her mouth work and quickly stood. "I didn't hear you pull up."

"That's because I walked."

It made her giddy—the fact that he lived close enough to get there by foot, that he'd been right around the corner from her all this time. The proximity presented so many options, for staying into the evening when they returned later on, their post-hike sweaty skin an invitation for getting even sweatier.

A suggestive smile slid over her face. "You might end up wishing you'd driven later on tonight. I heard it's supposed to rain."

Connor shrugged. "I don't have a car."

"Oh." She was momentarily thrown. How had he been getting into town and back? "I could have picked you up," she said, skipping down the steps to meet him.

Yes, she actually *skipped*.

Connor's grin widened as he fixed his eyes on her, his gaze making a lazy pass down her body and back up again. It made her feel like she was wearing lingerie instead of hiking gear. Or nothing at all.

"It wasn't a long walk," he said. "Ready to go?"

She had to remind herself that she really did want to go on this hike, and not try to convince him to go up to her bedroom and finish what they'd started instead.

They got into her car, and she handed him the map.

"Why don't you pick a trail?" she asked as she backed out the driveway.

"They're all pretty much the same to me, but sure."

"You don't have a preference?"

"Not really."

"I thought you wanted to hike?"

"No. *You* said you were hiking today. *I* just said I wanted to go with you." That impish grin of his flickered over his lips, lips that she knew the feel of, and Gabriella went hot inside.

She took them out of Portland, following the local streets she knew so well to I-295, the highway that would lead her south and to her future in a few weeks' time. For now, though, she turned north toward the comfort of the mountains. Connor played with the radio stations until he found a familiar song. When his arm stretched out over the gearshift, she caught a swirl of black ink by the edge of his sleeve.

"You didn't tell me you had a tattoo."

"You didn't ask," he said. "If it had been one of your questions last night, I might have."

"Well, we've got some time to keep playing now." They came to a red light, and she peeked down at his bicep. "Can I see it?"

Connor paused, then tugged up his shirtsleeve, revealing smooth, tanned skin that she itched to touch. The intricate design there, however, hijacked her attention. It was nearly an optical illusion, something that could have easily been confused with a tribal band, but it wasn't knot work at all. It was two dragons, both mirror images of one another, enmeshed together at tail and claw.

"It's beautiful," she said quietly. "What does it represent?"

Connor craned his neck, giving his arm a cursory glance before meeting Gabriella's eyes. "I guess I always thought it showed how everyone has two sides of themselves, both of them pulling at you at the same time. Or how we all have positive and negative experiences in life, and that brings us balance."

Connor's expression was serious, floating on the edge of the darkness she'd seen in them before, but then he grinned, his perfect white teeth gleaming.

"But the dude who did the tat just said it was two cool dragons."

Gabriella laughed and brought her focus back to the road. "I have one too, you know."

"Oh yeah?" He turned toward her, leaning over the gearshift. "What is it?"

"A butterfly," she replied. "Typical, I know."

Connor chuckled. "Typical you. It's duality."

She smiled, shocked at how well he seemed to know her

already. But then Connor leaned a little closer to her, and his voice went low and sexy when he asked, "Where is it?"

Her nipples stiffened as she imagined him drinking in the skin at the crease of her thigh. "Is one of the rules of this game that we have to answer the questions the other asks?"

"I don't think we came up with any rules."

"Well then, maybe I'll let you look for it later."

She may have sounded like she was teasing, but she couldn't have been more serious, ready for him to strip her clothes off on the trail, someplace hidden in the shadows of the trees.

"I'll try to be patient."

The light changed and she merged onto the highway, relaxing as they listened to the music and watched the scenery pass by. Lush summer pines lined the side of the road, interspersed with maples and aspens. Gabriella thought of how brilliantly they change colors in the fall, what they look like closer to Christmas, when snow weighed down their barren branches, embracing them in white. Maybe this year she'd come back over winter break, if her parents hadn't been able to sell the house yet. Or maybe Connor could come down to visit her at school. It was crazy, this hope that whatever they were becoming would last even after summer's heat faded into a memory, but maybe crazy was what she needed right now.

She took the exit at Freeport and slowed down at the crush of cars, the tourists hunting for parking by the outlets. When they reached Pownal and the gentle slope of the mountain, Gabriella let out a relieved sigh. She got out of the car and looked up at the sky through the canopy of leaves, breathing in the scent of bark and forest. She slipped her backpack over her arms while Connor looked at the map.

"Did you choose a path?"

"I think I'll use the tried and true, eenie-meanie-miney-moe strategy and pick..." He poked his finger against a random fold on the map. "This one."

Gabriella laughed, more at ease than she'd felt in months. Years, maybe. That dip above Connor's lip beckoned, and she wanted to throw her arms around him, to draw him close and kiss him silly as they began the ascent up the South Ridge Trail.

It was quiet and serene once they were safely nestled within the dense wood. The cool, still air was a stark contrast to the salty sea breeze and rush of wave against rock on the shore. The moss-covered ground and weathered boulders were distant cousins of the sandy coastline and sturdy lighthouses they'd left behind for the day. Connor reached out to take her hand. His fingers were warm and felt good wrapped around hers. They were halfway up the incline when he paused by a tremendous tree, its bark aged and gray. Its roots spindled down like veins over the obstinate surface of a large stone.

"Amazing how that happens, isn't it? That the roots can reach around anything in its way to seek out soil?"

He took their joined fingers and caressed the trunk, face lost in complete wonderment.

"I always thought part of the beauty of nature was in its common sense," Gabriella reasoned. "The tree is just doing what it needs to do in order to survive."

"But it shouldn't be able to. It's another example proving that the theory you're working so hard against."

"You're just hell bent on seeing me fail, aren't you?"

Connor pulled her toward another tree deeper in the thicket, a few feet away from the trail. He led her through the brush, and Gabriella enjoyed the feeling of secrecy it held.

"I don't want you to fail, but come on, even Buddhism recognizes the dual nature of things. How else can you explain yin and yang?"

"Are you a computer geek or an Eastern philosopher?"

"Can't I be both? You were the one who said I'm more than I seem." Connor stopped walking and turned to face her, searching her eyes, his free hand reaching up to cup her face. "You're so much more too."

He looked at her for a moment, his thumb stroking over her cheek. Then he kissed her gently, sweetly, his palm slipping down from her cheek to the back of her neck. There was nothing urgent about the kiss, and Gabriella let her eyes close, let herself fall into it, enjoying soft and tender in a way she never had before.

With a smile against his lips, she murmured, "Maybe I'll let you look for that butterfly now."

He skimmed his nose along hers. "Oh yeah? Here in the woods?"

"Here in the woods."

"Kinky." His touch traveled down her neck and over her shoulder. "Am I getting warm?"

"Freezing cold."

He touched her shoulder blades, her spine, the small of her back. "Warmer?"

"I'd say you're...temperate."

He chuckled. This time, the sound slid between her thighs. "You gonna give me a hint?"

Gabriella stood on her toes to whisper in his ear, "Lower."

Connor slipped his hands to her bottom, and her hard exhale was as loud as his hiss when he squeezed. His lips brushed hers in an open-mouthed tease. "Am I hot yet?"

"Almost." She reached back and drew one of his hands around to her belly. "Other side."

Connor groaned and pulled her to him with the hand still grabbing her ass. He fell back against a nearby tree, leaning on it for support, and Gabriella licked the shell of his ear. Reveling in his shudder, she bit down on his earlobe and brought his hand down toward the waistband of her shorts. She popped the first button open for him, and Connor's hand slipped inside.

"Now you're burning up," she told him.

"Fuck," he said, his breathing hard and fast. When his fingers stroked over the damp fabric covering her slit, he seemed to completely forget about his quest. Instead, he simply snapped.

Connor twisted her around until her back was shoved against the tree. He freed his hand from her shorts long enough to yank her shirt up, pulling it over her head. She raised her arms to help him, wrenching it off her wrists and throwing it to the ground. She tried to do the same to him, gripping the hem of his T-shirt and lifting it until her palms met the smooth, bare planes of his chest. Connor pulled back and whipped the shirt off, then kissed her again, sucking and biting as he worked to undo the remaining buttons on her shorts. It was wild and fast and risky and wrong, and she'd never felt so good in her life. She was about to beg him to go lower again, to soothe that wet ache between her legs when she heard voices. It was children's laughter, getting closer by the second.

Connor froze and reached frantically for their shirts. He picked them up and raised his arms to the tree's branches, his bulky frame and muscled arms hiding her from view. He kept watch over his shoulder, waiting for the family to pass.

Gabriella grinned, dizzy with the satisfaction of finally seeing how far he was willing to go. It was a given that they weren't going to be alone out here, but she didn't want to stop. There were other spots along the mountain where they could hide, places where they could be alone and forget the roles they'd been forced to play. She wanted to let him finish looking for that butterfly, to find the hottest places inside her and not stop until they were both shaking.

The children disappeared with their parents down the path. Connor turned back to face her, his head lowered and eyes closed in obvious relief.

"Connor," she began, searching for the right way to tell him what she was feeling.

You're so much more than I'd hoped.

You're everything I've been waiting for.

"I shouldn't have done that," he said.

Gabriella shook her head, but with his eyes still closed, Connor didn't see it. He must have thought that she was humiliated, not thrilled that he nearly just made one of her longest running fantasies a reality.

"No, Connor, it's—"

"I know. I was out of line. We went too far. It was completely inappropriate."

Gabriella paused, the crushing weight of disappointment coming down like a chokehold, the things she was about to say caught in her throat. Connor opened his eyes and handed her back her shirt.

"It was wrong," he added, nodding at words that didn't even sound like his, face stern and unreadable.

It was wrong.

The words fed into all her past rejections, Gabriella's self-doubt clamping down her jaw and stinging her eyes with tears. She wanted to scream, to tell him that he was the one who was wrong. That out of line and inappropriate were exactly what she'd been starving for. But she couldn't bear to tell him that and see the same look of disgust and shock in his eyes that she'd seen too many times before. So she let her rational side take the driver's seat, mirrored Connor's nod and forced out a cool, calm reply.

"It's all right."

Without meeting his eyes, she carefully rebuttoned her shorts and put her shirt back on.

Connor kicked at the ground. "Do you want to keep going?"

She nodded again, although she wasn't sure if he was asking about the hike or the crumbling beginnings of their would-be love affair. Both of them were ruined now, anyway.

They wordlessly trekked up to the mountain's peak and sat for a few minutes on the flat expanse of rock. As they looked out over the horizon, Connor kept a healthy distance between them, not even coming close enough to let their fingertips touch. All at once, he appeared no different from every other man she'd been with: closed off, hesitant and restrained. It made her feel sick to her stomach. They picked their way back down the mountain without speaking, and by the time they returned to her car, she couldn't wait to get home.

They remained silent for the drive back to Portland. Outside, the sky was getting cloudy, overcast and gray. They were passed by a group of motorbikes on the highway, flying by her in the left lane. In a moment of desperation, she sought out her masked rider, but every one of them was dressed in bright blues and red racing stripes. There were no traces of his slick, dark leather or his shiny black bike anywhere.

Gabriella pulled robotically onto her driveway. The quiet in the car was stifling.

"So I'll call you later?" Connor asked, tentative even in the way he angled his body toward her in the passenger seat. "There's a bonfire down at the beach tonight."

"Sure," she lied. "Sounds great."

She flipped through the excuses that came to her mind.

I just don't feel the same way.

I have to focus on my studies.

But it hurt to think of saying things like that to him.

He walked her to her front door, and she ducked away from the kiss he tried to place on her cheek. She had to turn away from the hurt she saw in his eyes.

"I'm sorry," he whispered as she went inside.

It was the same thing she would have said too.

TEN

Connor walked until the late afternoon hours fell into dusk. The brilliantly sunny day had faded into a chilly summer rain, the kind that didn't so much come down from the clouds but seemed to saturate the air in every direction. It was fitting—the gloom was the ideal accompaniment to his epic state of fuckup.

Today had been amazing. Being with Gabby and so far away from Portland and his past, he felt more free than he could ever remember being. He'd never really thought about it before, but he'd always been fascinated by nature, the way leaves and flowers kept coming back no matter how badly winter beat the crap out of them, year after year. Nature was a survivor, just like him. Surrounded by those trees and the way Gabby looked at him, he got lost in it. Got lost in her.

How could he not have? She seemed to see through him, to not even notice the shell of his former life he thought followed him everywhere like a ghost. She'd said there was more to him than his closest friends realized, even after only knowing him a few days. Somehow, she saw *him*. He had to show her what that meant to him, and how incredible he thought she was too. The idea of losing that moment, of letting her walk out of the forest without telling her exactly how amazing she was, was something he couldn't let happen.

But apparently, that was yet another phenomenal joke.

He'd wanted it to be special, and all he ended up doing was maul her against a tree. He couldn't stop himself. All it took was the feel of the bare skin of her belly and the damp, soft cotton of her panties, and he lost control. She'd made him want to be different, but in the end, he couldn't. He'd tried to replace himself with a better version, with his opposite, and it didn't change a goddamn thing. He'd never be able to fix things with her. Not after today.

Connor felt that same tension from his childhood balling up in his stomach again—the feeling like he had to fight the whole goddamn world just to get a scrap of happiness.

He kept walking until he hit the strip of beach by the cove, his hands firmly entrenched in his pockets. His shirt was wet, his hair was sticking to his forehead, and his socks were soaked through, but he didn't care. He just stood there and looked out at the murky horizon, almost unable to make out where the line of the ocean met the dreary clouds. The weather hadn't stopped a bunch of kids from setting up camp at the water's edge, though. Connor watched as they hovered around a spot in the sand and then suddenly jumped back, running with their heads turned to look over their shoulders as the firework they'd just lit exploded into the air. As it fizzled to the ground, one of the kids punched a fist above his head in glee. They all ran back to where they'd started, skidding to their knees in the wet sand to light another. They were too busy and the ocean was too loud for them to hear the sound of tires rolling over the pavement, but Connor knew what was behind him before he even turned around.

The Cumberland County patrol car crept up the concrete, silent and predatory. The cop inside it wasn't looking at him, but

Connor froze even though he hadn't done a damn thing. His throat clamped shut, his reaction Pavlovian—a response ingrained in him after years of encountering men in uniform bearing unfriendly faces. He could see each one of them in that set of headlights, in the engine that idled in the rain, the wipers that slowly canvassed the windshield: the cops who had carted him back home after his first break-in, his second and his third. The investigator who looked at their ratty apartment with blatant scorn when Patricia reported Travis missing. The cruiser he'd sat handcuffed in when he'd stolen his grandfather's car. Sheriff Roger and his sneer from the other side of the bars as Connor sat in a cell.

That was who Connor really was. He could hide from his past for a time, pretend he'd left it all behind him, but it was still there. It didn't matter how far he'd taken things with Gabby today. Eventually, the truth about the past would have come out, and he would have lost her anyway.

Another firework screamed into the air by the shore, and the cop bolted out of the car. Connor turned on his heel, knowing his shot to get the hell outta Dodge when he saw it. He kept his eyes on the ground and the wet gravel that spat up under his feet, his shoulders bunched up by his ears as he found his way home.

"We were waiting for you."

Connor looked up. His grandmother was sitting on the porch swing. She had a pile of knitting on her lap.

Dinner. Of course. Crap.

"Sorry, I lost track of time." He reached for the door. "I'll get started on the dishes—"

She held up a hand to stop him. "I've already got your grandfather on that. Go change out of those wet clothes and come back here."

She was using that tone again, the one he didn't dare defy. With a sigh, Connor went into his room and twisted off his drenched clothing. He hadn't realized how soaked he was until he was finally in warm, dry clothes again.

The rain had finally let up when he returned to the porch, the sky clearing just in time to showcase the purple glow of the sunset. His grandmother nodded to the spot next to her on the swing. Connor sank down onto it.

"I know that look," she said.

"What look?"

"The one you've got on your face right now. It's the look of a man who's regretting something."

He winced. "Grandma, I—"

"I don't need the details, and I'm sure you don't want to tell me them, either. So sum it up. Ten words or less."

Connor closed his eyes. Opened them again. Bent his head back and stared at the part of the roof that hung over the porch. Out of the corner of his eye, he saw his grandmother calmly resume her knitting. Her movements seemed to say, *any time, now.*

"I tried to be someone else," he finally said. "But I couldn't."

She dropped her knitting to her lap. "Why would you ever try to do that?"

"I couldn't let Gabby know the person I used to be."

"Who were you, then?"

He swallowed. "Someone I thought she deserved."

She sighed, a heavy sound of someone who'd been a parent once already and was too old to have to do it all over again. Guilt ate at Connor like a festering wound but then she said, "You know, just because your parents made the choices they did, it doesn't mean you aren't worthy of love."

Her words cut right through him, a gut punch that left him short of breath. It took a minute before he could reply.

"I wanted her to think I was, but I couldn't take the risk. I had to be someone different."

"You're acting like there are only two options. That Connor or this one. Black or white. One or zero."

His brow shot up at her mention of binary language. She didn't flinch.

"That's right, I actually know a thing or two about technology." She smiled and picked up her knitting again. His eyes followed the movement of the needles, loop by loop. "No one is all one thing, honey, and I'm betting your Gabriella isn't either."

Something about the idea of her being *his Gabriella* made Connor's chest go tight with wanting.

"I thought I was doing the right thing," he said.

"You're never doing the right thing if you're not being yourself. But you've always been like that, ever since you showed up at our door. It's like that quote you have tacked to your desk at work. 'Make an island of yourself, make yourself your refuge.' You've tried to be an island, not needing anyone, but that doesn't work for very long. Eventually, we need someone to see us for who we are."

His gut twisted again, this time not with the waves of anger or resentment he'd come to know so well. He didn't recognize the feeling at first, but he thought it was something that resembled hope.

An engine rattled down the road. Connor looked up to see Dean pulling up in front of his house, a pile of driftwood in the back of the truck. The bonfire. He'd forgotten all about it. He'd agreed to go when he thought Gabby might go with him. Maybe there was a chance she still would, and he could come clean, and they could start over again.

He turned back to his grandmother. "Do you need me to—"

"Go."

He kissed her cheek and leapt down the steps, palming his

phone as he walked to the curb. He got into the passenger seat and dialed Gabby's number.

"Where's your girl?" Dean asked.

She didn't pick up. The call went to voicemail. "Just drive."

He still hadn't reached her an hour later, when they'd built up the driftwood into a plume of orange that crackled against the night sky. He must have tried her number every fifteen minutes, but she wasn't answering.

Connor shoved his phone into his pocket, walked over to the abandoned lifeguard stand pushed up tight against the dunes and looked around. The scene in front of him was one he'd been a part of too many times before. In the parking lot, a strange mix of country and hip hop blasted from competing cars' speakers. A keg sat at the back of someone's SUV. Dean had disappeared shortly after they'd gotten there, and was most likely wrapped up in a beach towel with God knows who.

Connor wanted Gabby like that, here with him. He wanted her giggling as he tugged her away from the crowd, wanted to press her down in the night-cooled sand. To see if all of her skin glowed the way her face did, shining in the moonlight that bounced off the waves. To get her so hot that she lost all sense of modesty or control, get her even more frantic and desperate than she seemed to be every time they were together.

He thought about her then, how she'd been more than willing to push things a step further. The way she'd unbuttoned his jeans on the dock, and her hitched breath as she found the stiff shape of him inside. How she'd pleaded for more in the tent at the park. The hike, and how she'd taken his hand and pushed it into her shorts.

Could Gabby be different from the girl he'd imagined?

He was sure it had all been him, so absolutely certain that she'd want someone different from who he was, but she'd been just as eager as him whenever they were alone. The things he'd said about his behavior being out of line and inappropriate were what he thought Gabby would want to hear, but the truth was she'd told him she wanted to be bad. That good was overrated. That she didn't want him to behave. And she seemed to have no problem getting down and dirty in public. As a matter of fact, not only did she like it, she begged him for it, even when only shadows and some poorly constructed fabric hid them from the eyes of everyone around.

Connor wanted to make her beg. To coerce her into telling him about her dirtiest fantasies then act them all out. He wanted to let loose with her, to show her the side of him he'd kept on lockdown.

Maybe he didn't have to try so hard to be someone else for her. Maybe he could actually be himself.

He called her again, but no dice.

Tomorrow. He would go to her house tomorrow. Then he'd let himself be the version of Connor he really was and tell her everything.

ELEVEN

By the time Gabriella kicked off her blanket the next morning after a lousy night's sleep, she was angry at the world. At her mother for demanding so much of her only daughter, and her father for barely being a part of her life. At Nana for telling her to be true to herself, when it was a feat that obviously was completely impossible. Her fury extended to her M.I.T. peers and their complacent acceptance of life without passion. To Kevin, and all the ex-boyfriends before him, who never gave her what she needed. She could kill Jamie for bringing Connor into her life. And as for Connor Starks? Well, damn him too for having been so close to what she thought she wanted. What she *knew* she wanted. He dangled it in front of her and then took it away without any explanation as to why. And, in that moment, she couldn't stay quiet about what she wanted anymore.

Gabriella put on her glasses, stomped across the floor and grabbed her phone. It was warm from where it had sat charging on her desk, baking in the early morning sunlight. She didn't bother to check the string of calls she'd missed—they were all probably from Jamie, harassing her for going off the map.

She began typing an email to Connor that fringed on the edges of madness, although she was sure it was just the caffeine deprivation and lack of sleep. She told him that another person lived and breathed inside the one she appeared to be—the one who got the perfect grades and wanted the career. That she hungered for someone to be as wild and reckless as she wanted to be. For a man to hold what she wanted at bay until she was desperate and shaking and begging, the way he did to her on the dock and in the park. Her words rambled on, streams of consciousness unbefitting of a PhD candidate, but she kept going nonetheless. Her hands shook as she wrote that if he felt what happened on the hike was wrong, then she didn't want to waste any more of his time. That it wouldn't work, that he shouldn't call her again, and that she was sorry too.

She hit send and immediately felt dazed, as if she'd been released from a long imprisonment, but she was still trapped. Because what difference did it make if Connor knew what she wanted? He obviously didn't want the same thing.

Gabriella splashed some water on her face, mechanically brushed her teeth and hair, and stumbled downstairs to the kitchen. Despite wearing nothing but her tank top and pajama shorts, sweat bloomed over her skin. The air was sticky and hot, with no land breeze to offset the humidity. She wrenched open the fridge door and stood in front of it in an attempt to cool off. It didn't help.

Then a distant rumble caught her attention.

No. She couldn't. She just couldn't take seeing him now. Her masked rider, like Connor, was everything she couldn't have and shouldn't have wanted. Part of her longed to turn away and hide, but the rest was consumed by her insatiable curiosity, wanting to watch all that power and heat race by.

Unable to help herself, she turned from the fridge and crept to the front door, pushing it open as the sound of the bike's roar grew louder. He turned the corner, slowed and came to a stop in between her house and Jamie's.

Her heart slammed against her rib cage, her breathing tight and shallow. Her brain sputtered through questions about what he was doing out so early, when the sun had barely tipped past the edges of the shore, and why he was *here*. Her limbs locked in place, she stared as he cut the bike's engine, the air between them seeming to bend in the simmering heat. But then she noticed something different about him. He wasn't wearing his leather riding jacket or gloves—all he had on was a white tank top and jeans. Golden muscles gleamed with sweat beneath the shorn edges of his shirt. And surrounding his left arm was a tribal-looking tattoo.

Connor's tattoo.

Gabriella started to panic, feeling slightly sick as she watched him dismount and pull off his helmet. His dark hair was wet, sticking to his forehead and neck as if he were fresh from a shower. He dropped the helmet onto the seat and glared at her. His perfect face was filled with anger.

She clutched the screen door, clinging to it as if her legs had suddenly become useless and it was the only thing holding her up. He silently peeled open her grandmother's gate and stalked toward her. His boots fell heavy on the porch steps, his eyes burning into hers as he loomed in front of her, all man and muscle and sweat. He was as lethal and fierce as she'd always imagined her rider would be, and Gabriella was too awestruck, too confused and embarrassed to know what to say.

"You were going to dump me in an email?"

"I...I thought you didn't drive."

"I said I didn't have a car," Connor spat out. His upper lip twitched, his eyes flashing. "Fixing bikes was my old job. I rebuilt this one myself. And don't change the subject."

He took another step closer. Gabriella couldn't move. The

tension between them was menacing. It was her fantasy come to life, but all wrong.

"You weren't even going to talk to me?" he demanded. "I should just never call you again? Pretend like this week didn't mean anything?"

She backed inside the house and he followed, letting the screen door bang shut behind him as she stumbled back into the kitchen. She had to turn away from him—she couldn't bear to see him like that, with his stare so wild and angry and cutting into her. She dropped her head and braced her palms on the counter.

"I'm sorry. I thought you didn't..." she stammered. "I just wanted—"

"You think I felt what happened between us was wrong? You couldn't tell how crazy it was making me, wanting you like this?"

He moved in behind her, and his closeness stole her words. Connor pushed his body flush behind hers, and Gabriella's mouth fell open. It was fear and relief and a fierce kind of wanting all mixed together. She could feel every line of his body, every hard drag of muscle. His mouth was at her ear, his face sweaty, and she reeled at the sensation of his hot breath, his damp skin and stubble rasping along her neck. He took her hands in his and forcefully anchored them to the countertop.

"You want to know what it feels like to lose control, Gabby? Well, now's your opportunity. Here's your last chance to say no."

She couldn't say no, couldn't say anything at all. She simply writhed against his implacable form when he bit down on the junction between her shoulder and neck, sucking hard on the skin there. She whimpered, and Connor chuckled as he shoved her forward harder, trapping her between his body and the counter.

"That's what I thought," he growled. "Do. Not. Move."

He released her wrists, and she had no time to process it all, to consider how she was about to be taken, before his fingers slipped into her top. He found her nipple and stroked his thumb over it as the palm of his other hand covered the space below her navel, fingers spanning to create the most delicious pressure. His thick length jutted out hard in his jeans, and she ground back against him, greedy for more. But even with his body holding hers prisoner, Gabriella was still pissed off. Why didn't he tell her who he really was? Why had he held back all this time, instead of doing this?

"Is that all you've got?" she challenged. "Is that the best you can do?"

Connor moved quickly to her side and braced both of his legs on either side of her thigh. She'd only just registered the movement when his hand came down, fast and stinging on her rear. She grunted, a lewd noise that left her throat raspy and raw.

"You want more? You want it rough and dirty, just like I do?"

He punctuated his words with another smack, and she cried out from the sharp twist of pain and pleasure that ricocheted through her body, from the feeling of *finally*. Of *yes*.

"Is that what you want, Miss Ivy League? You want me to turn your ass red?"

"Fuck—" Another smack. "Yes. I want that."

"Open your legs wider."

She complied, and he bent her farther over the countertop, holding her in place as he landed a swift blow to the sweet spot between her thighs. She choked out a sound that was a gasp and a groan at the same time. She couldn't believe how good it felt. Connor slid his hand under the elastic of her pajama bottoms, fingers riding down the curve of her ass until he found the stretch of fabric that had surpassed damp long ago. He pressed and stroked, making her curse when his middle finger rubbed against the sopping cotton.

"I knew it. I knew you'd be drenched for me."

She turned to glower at him. "What have you been waiting for, then?"

Connor glared back. The look in his eyes was defiance, fury and sex all rolled up into one. He moved behind her again, shoved his free hand into her hair and wrenched her head back. It shouldn't have felt so good to be overpowered that way, but fuck, it did.

"I *waited* because I thought it was the right thing to do. Because I was trying to be a gentleman." He released her hair, and Gabriella almost lost her balance as he wrestled her shorts and panties down her legs. "I was waiting on the pier when I really wanted to taste you. Waiting at the park, when I wanted to push my fingers inside you and make you scream louder than the fireworks."

She groaned with the thought of his restraint. He grabbed her by the hips and turned her around to face him. With one swift move, he hurled her up onto the countertop, her thighs sweaty as they skidded over the Formica. Connor tugged her clothes from her, throwing them to the floor, and she trembled as he stared her down, fingers at her waist hard enough to bruise.

"You have no idea what you do to me. How hard it's been to behave myself around you. But I'm through with being good. I don't want to wait anymore."

He grasped her by the knees and shoved her legs apart, eyes blazing as he bent down, his mouth open in an erotic promise. Then he extended his tongue and slowly licked up her slit. Gabriella gasped and clenched her eyes shut.

"Oh, no you don't," he rasped. "Eyes open."

She managed to obey, only to have her lids start to sink shut again at the image of Connor's wicked smirk between her legs. He cupped the sticky skin behind her knees and pried her legs wider, opening her up even further to him.

"That's right. Eyes on me."

He licked again and started up a rhythm, alternating between soft, easy strokes, taut flicks, and grazing his teeth over her clit.

"Fuck fuck fuck," she chanted, gripping the edges of the counter. He delved his tongue lower, thrusting it inside her, and Gabriella twisted sharply, ripples of pleasure shooting up her spine.

"Don't stop," she whimpered.

Connor chuckled, his breath warm against her skin. Those big hands of his found her ass and dragged her toward him, fingers wide as he spread her cheeks apart.

"Oh my God, are you going to..." She sank back onto her elbows, watching that evil gleam in his eyes flare even brighter before his face disappeared from view. "No one's ever...oh *shit*."

He lapped at the puckered hole that no one before him had ever touched, and it sent an electric current straight through her. Her legs jerked, head snapping back on a gasp. Needing something to anchor her, she reached for his hair with both hands, spearing her fingers into it as his tongue danced a wet path around her back entrance. It was so intense, so perfectly perverse that she almost tried to wriggle away, but he kept a tight hold on her, lifting his head and forcing her still.

"You'd better be sure you want this, baby girl, because I'm not going to stop now. I'm going to fuck you senseless. In every room in this house. So hard you'll still be feeling my cock in you tomorrow. And you're going to scream so loud the whole damn neighborhood is going to know how good you're getting fucked."

"I want it," she moaned, loving the raw desire in his words. He closed his eyes and returned to her clit, no longer teasing, his lips and tongue forming a rhythmic suction that brought her orgasm front and center. He added two fingers to the mix, driving them in her pussy.

"*Fuck*, yes." She sounded like an animal, and she loved it.

"You like that?" He added a third finger, plunging them deep, making her arch and groan. "Tell me. Do you like me fucking you with my fingers here in your grandmother's kitchen, with all the windows open so anyone could hear?"

"God, yes."

"I bet you're riding my fingers the way you want to ride my cock."

The image set off a powder keg inside her. "Fuck, please. I want your cock so bad."

Connor's breathing suddenly went harsh. His eyes flew open, fingers sliding free, strong hands pulling her off the counter and spinning her around. Her knees were too wobbly to keep her up. Her legs gave out and she sagged back against him, but Connor was right there behind her, pulling her limp body up along his. His mouth at her ear again, he glided his hand over her hip, leaving a trail of her moisture on her skin.

"You want that? You want my cock, baby girl?"

"Yes," she whined.

She could feel his lips spreading into a grin. "That's what I thought."

Gabriella dropped her head and watched him palm her belly, his hand inching lower until he parted her folds with one finger and began rubbing her already sensitive clit. He circled and stroked, his touch skimming over that perfect spot *right there* until she was teetering on the edge, chasing the kind of shattering relief she'd been desperate to know.

"You're gonna make me come."

"Oh no. You're not coming yet. Not until I get inside you." He slowed his movements, edging her back down, and nipped at her earlobe. "Table, Gabby. Walk. *Now.*"

Somehow she found a way to put one foot in front of the other while he continued to torture her, never letting up the slow circles he drew over her wet flesh. Her orgasm was starting to crest again by the time they finally reached the table

—she could barely hold it off—but then he pulled his hand away.

"Oh please." She could hear how pitiful she sounded, but she didn't care.

"Turn around. Get up on top."

She did as she was told and shimmied up onto the polished wood. Connor clutched the bottom of her top and dragged it up over her head, then bent down to capture one pert nipple between his lips. He flicked his tongue over the beaded tip, pinching and rolling the other between two fingers. The sensation sent a shockwave down to where she was achingly empty.

"Want you," she breathed. "Now."

She reached over the wide expanse of his shoulders and clawed at his tank until her palms met the ropy muscles of his back. She tried to pull the shirt off him, but she couldn't with his mouth still driving her crazy. He stood up and quickly ripped the tank from his body. Gabriella greedily raked her nails down his torso, licking her lips as she traced the soft trail of hair that disappeared inside his jeans. She kissed him then, as hard as he'd kissed her, and fumbled with his belt, trying to tear it open.

Connor moaned into her mouth and yanked her hands away, silver clanging as he did the job for her. "God, you're so hot. I can't fucking stand it."

He stripped down his jeans and boxers, freeing his cock. It was so smooth, so thick and long. She wanted to wrap her fingers around it, to watch his eyes roll back and his jaw go slack, to take him in her mouth and tease him until he was out of his mind too. His boots thumped to the floor as he kicked them off and stepped out of his pants before lunging forward again. He claimed her mouth, teeth clashing against hers as he fumbled with something in between their bodies.

Condom.

The thought registered, and Connor broke the kiss, looking down as he ripped the foil package open. Gabriella whimpered and rocked her hips against the table.

"Jesus, I love the sounds you make," he said. "Lie down. Hands above your head."

She complied, raising her arms up as she watched him sheath himself. When he'd rolled the condom all the way down, he wrapped one hand around each of her thighs and jerked her toward him until her legs were split open obscenely wide on either side of his hips. But he still didn't give her what she wanted. No, he simply slid that swollen, ridged head back and forth over her throbbing clit, never once breaking eye contact.

"You wanted someone wild and reckless?" he asked. "You wanted to be desperate, shaking and begging?"

She mewled, nodding wildly at the words he was repeating from her email.

"Are you desperate for me now, Gabby? Are you shaking?"

She couldn't reply, not with his cock stroking over her like that, so close to where she needed it. Her head sank back on its stem, but Connor gathered her hair in one hand and forced her to look up at him.

"Beg me."

God, she loved it. The command in his voice. The way his lip curled. The unwavering look in his eyes. The feeling of being completely carried away. Even as she was ready to scream in frustration, she knew he was everything she'd ever wanted.

"Please, *please*, fuck me, Connor. I can't take it anymore."

He let go of her hair and drew his hips back, looking down as he lined himself up, then stopped and glanced at her thigh. With a grin, he leaned in and whispered, "I found your butterfly, baby girl."

Before she could answer, Connor fucked into her in one deep, long thrust. Her head sank back as she gave into the fullness, the burning stretch, that sweet hot ache. He trembled and held himself still for a moment, pinching his eyes shut. She watched the muscles in his neck and shoulders bunch and cord, that perfect face of his melting into a grimace of pleasure.

"Gabby, fuck. You feel fucking amazing."

He pulled out an inch at a time, unbearably slow. She dug her heels into his ass, trying to stop him, to coax him back inside her, but he shook his head with a grin, his strength dominating as he found his composure. He took his time until she could only feel the tip of him, then eased into her pussy again. Out slowly, back in. Gabriella writhed beneath him, her hips curving up toward his deliberate, unhurried thrusts. Then he did something different, changed his angle somehow and rubbed against a spot inside her that made her absolutely sure she was going to die.

"Oh, God...do that again."

He did, and it was almost too much. A third time and she was begging him not to stop. Connor groaned, his forehead bowed and pressed against her neck. She heard something catch in his breathing, like he'd almost just given in, but he lifted himself up, bracketing her between his arms and picking up his pace, fucking her hard and fast, just as he'd promised. He drove her to the edge and kept her there, and she couldn't take another second.

She brought a hand down between her thighs and started to stroke. She could only imagine what she looked like, mouth open, eyes glazed, defiant and triumphant. But Connor knocked her hand away and drew her arm back up over her head.

"Don't you dare. I'm the one who's gonna make you scream."

He licked the pad of his thumb and brought it down to her clit, rubbing it in swift little circles.

"Oh please." She clutched his forearms as her legs lifted and started to shake, but even with white-hot pleasure bearing down on her, she couldn't let go.

"Come on. Show me, Gabby. Show me what a freaky little slut you can be. Let me see what you look like when you come."

His words reached inside her, a balm over everything that had felt so broken and wrong. It was the key to unlocking that latch, and she gave in, releasing the dirty, sexual side to her she'd kept locked up for so long.

"Connor...Connor, fuck—" Her voice broke as her orgasm took hold with a shattering force she couldn't control, didn't want to control, her whole body thrashing, head slamming back on the table.

"That's right," he murmured. "There you go."

The sultry approval in his voice and the relentless circling of his thumb sent her into a surprising second and even harder release, and she bucked up against him, crying out until her throat went raspy from her screams.

Connor gave in then—she felt it as the breath rushed out of him, his thrusts turning erratic and jerky. He slid his arms under her until his fingers dug into her shoulders and pounded fiercely into her, burying his face against her neck. He stilled and choked out a gasp, moaning her name, and the sound of it nearly got her started all over again.

Calmed but short of breath, Connor looked up at her. His hair was damp on his forehead, his eyes hooded.

"Still want to dump me?"

Panting, she shook her head. "No."

"Good. Because I'm not nearly finished with you yet."

TWELVE

Hours later, they somehow made it up to her bedroom, and Gabriella felt sore and used in a way she never had before. After they'd recovered from their activities in the dining room, Connor led her outside, carrying her when she'd squealed in protest. Logically, there was no reason she should have objected. After all, this was what she had been waiting for.

He'd laid her down in the grass that sat in the shadow of her grandmother's rose bushes and kissed every inch of her, her soft sighs getting carried away on the breeze. Connor reverently caressed the butterfly drawn on her hip, running his lips over it before sliding down to lap at where she was still surprisingly ready for more.

His tongue searched out the places on her body that were freshly fucked, and she grew hungry for the feel of him in her mouth. Pulling off her glasses, she tugged him by his shoulders until he'd rotated around, his torso over her, his knees on either side of her head. He lowered himself slowly, cock probing her mouth with gentle thrusts, but Gabriella wanted none of that. She grabbed him by the hips and drew him deep into her throat, relishing the groan that vibrated through him. She lost her rhythm for a second when he started working his magic with his mouth, needing a second to absorb the sensation that barreled through her before she could concentrate on him again.

They worked each other like that, sounds of pleasure meshing with birdsong and the rustling breeze until they were both shuddering in the sun-warmed grass.

After that, he took her back inside and asked her where the shower was.

In the cocoon of her steam-filled bathroom, Connor washed the traces of brown and green from her skin and then folded them both into a large towel, drying them off. She couldn't find a T-shirt of her own big enough for him, but he was content going commando under her blanket. The idea of him naked in her bed would have been enough to drive her crazy, but their morning adventures had left her satisfied.

For the time being.

Gabriella donned a tank top and a pair of panties, putting her glasses back on before settling down next to him. He splayed one arm out across her pillow, palm up in a silent invitation. It somehow seemed more intimate than all the things they'd done. She rested her head on his chest and stretched her body out alongside his. When he started playing with her hair, it was like her whole body went limp. She'd never felt so relaxed, so safe, and all this with her rider, the man she'd fantasized about all summer. She wrapped her arms around him and sighed.

"You okay, Gabby?"

She peeked up at him. "Why do you call me that?"

His hand paused in her hair. "It seemed to fit you better."

It was an answer that made sense. She could be content with that. She smiled and stared at the dip above his upper lip until she could no longer resist. She reached up, tentative at first, and then stroked the tip of her finger over it. The taunting little indentation was just as smooth as she imagined.

He laughed and captured her finger in his hand. "What are you doing?"

"I've wanted to touch that spot above your lip since we met. It's been tormenting me, wondering what it felt like."

"And was it all you were hoping for?"

Everything and more.

"It was."

But there was another thing that had been torturing her since he rolled up on her driveway. As if he could sense the shift in her mood, he let her finger go. She took the opportunity to trace it along his tattoo.

"Why didn't you tell me you had a motorcycle? I've only been staring at you the whole summer." She thought back to their first date, and how her rider had nearly run her over before she got there. Her eyes went wide. "Oh my God, that was *you* on the street by the coffee shop."

Connor laughed. His boyish smile returned.

"You weren't the only one watching someone," he said. "I sped up so I could see you before I had to go on this awful blind date. I really didn't want to go, but I'm glad I gave in to Jamie's badgering." He caressed her cheek. "It looks like she knew what she was doing."

"Wait—" She sat up, everything clicking into place. "Jamie knows you have a bike."

"Yeah..."

"And she knew you'd been watching me."

He shrugged, blushing slightly. "I probably wasn't as good at hiding it as I'd hoped."

Gabriella pinched her eyes shut, mouth dropping open as she shook her head. "I'm going to *kill* her." But she said it with laugher, amazed that Jamie not only never judged her, but had known what she'd wanted all along.

When she opened her eyes, Connor was giving her a look that made her pretty sure he thought she was going crazy. "Am I missing something?"

"No, it's just..." She stared at him, realization coming over her like the slow rush of the tide. It was crazy—the knowledge that he'd been her rider all along, watching her, wanting her. "Why didn't you tell me that was you when you got there? I would have jumped you right there in the coffee shop."

He laughed again, albeit a little more quietly, then swallowed and looked away, his jaw set tight. "I didn't want you to know. It's like I told you. I haven't always been the nicest guy."

He was so beautiful, those long eyelashes of his fanning over his cheeks, but she could feel the tension rolling off him. She snuggled closer and he pulled her against him, wrapping both arms around her. It seemed like he needed her near before he said anything more, like she was his lifeline, somehow.

"I don't have a good rep in this town, Gabby. I've been in trouble with the law. Done some seriously stupid shit. It's only in the past few years that I've cleaned up my act, and that's because my grandparents threatened holy hell on me if I didn't."

"I'm guessing we're talking more than just a few bad nights with the county sheriff."

Connor nodded. "I was so mad when my mom left. I took it out on everyone around me. I didn't care who I hurt. And, I, uh... I don't have the best track record with dating, either. I've done a lot of fucked up stuff without thinking. Slept with a lot of girls when I shouldn't have. Probably broken a few hearts, I don't know. I've never stuck around long enough with any of them to find out."

She laughed, amazed at just how much the two of them had in common. It must have seemed odd to him, because he angled his head and gave her that look again. Embarrassment gripped her for a moment, but after what they'd just shared, after how dirty they were together, she decided to give total honesty a go.

"I broke up with my last boyfriend because he couldn't find my clit."

Connor barked out a laugh. "Seriously?"

"Seriously. Every time it was like he was trying to map out the Andes, searching around with this look of utter concentration on his face. It was awful."

He laughed again, and this time she joined him. Then she shook her head and sighed.

"My parents wanted me to marry him. My mom was pissed when I broke it off. But it seems like no matter what I've done, all they've ever cared about is my ability to get a husband who looks good on paper, not about what makes me happy. It's part of why we aren't close. That and because they've just cut out my heart and put it on the market."

Connor frowned, his brow furrowed once again in confusion. She hadn't mentioned the impending sale to him before, unwilling to open up about something that cut so deep. But he'd accepted her so completely, drawn back the curtains over the part of herself she'd been trying to bury. Set free the sexual side that others had scorned. He'd shared the painful details of his own past too. There was no reason she couldn't do the same.

She could trust him, with her body and her heart.

"They're selling this house," she told him. "It's gonna kill me to let it go."

His frown deepened. "That's awful. Is there anything you can do to stop them?"

"I don't know." She'd played with the idea of going to a lawyer, but she didn't think she had a leg to stand on. "I wish they understood what this place means to me. When I was with Nana, I could just *be*, you know? No expectations. No disappointments. I never felt like that anywhere else. With my parents, my friends growing up, my boyfriends—no one seemed to get me. I always felt like this..." she shrugged, "...outcast. I hated trying to be who they wanted me to be, like I was forcing myself into a skin that didn't fit."

Connor reached up and ran his index finger over her earring.

"Is that why you did this?" His other hand stroked her ink. "And this?"

She grinned sheepishly. "I'm a little bit of a rebel too, you know."

"I'm getting the idea." He kissed her, his lips a gentle brush over hers. "So, we're both rebels. Could be a dangerous combination."

"Could be." She settled back down into the crook of his arm. "I wish you'd told me who you were from the start. You don't know how many fantasies I've had about being on the back of that bike with you. I could have been your riding buddy." She turned to face him, remembering another reason she'd watched him so intently. "Hey, why do you always ride alone? I mean, don't you biker guys come in packs?"

The awkward twist of his lips made her think she'd struck a chord she should have avoided.

"Dean doesn't ride. His truck is his baby. And Mikey would probably fall off one." Connor looked like he was trying to smile, but it wasn't working. He gave up. "My dad was the one who got me into bikes, before he left. And I guess it's easier to be alone. That way no one can ever get close to me again." He shook his head. "Cliché, I know."

Gabriella reached up and cupped his cheek. Connor glanced down at her hand with the strangest look on his face, like he didn't know how to react. Then he kissed her palm and brought it to his chest.

"I was sure if I let you know the real me, you'd run in the

other direction. Every time we were together, I thought I was just screwing up all over again. Taking things too far, and—"

Gabriella looked up at him, her hand still pressed over his heart. "And?"

He took a breath. "And I worried if we went too far, and then you got word about what a bad kid I was, you'd see the same shit the rest of this town does."

She pressed a kiss to his shoulder. "What did you think I would see?"

He lowered his chin and set his mouth in a firm line. "That I'm a loser. A fucked-up orphan who fixes up bikes and plays with computers, and doesn't have a shot in hell at being more."

His words broke her heart. She hated that he saw himself that way, when in such a short time being with him, she'd seen so much more to him than that.

"That's not who you are. It's not what I see," she said softly. "You can be the rebel who rides the bike, the programmer, the nature lover who spouts philosophy, and the man who does the filthiest things to me bare-ass naked in the backyard."

She smiled, hoping the last line would draw a laugh from him, but Connor was silent when he met her eyes. His stare was so intense it took her breath away.

"What?" she asked.

"You can be more than one thing too, you know."

Gabriella's chest started to constrict, all her old ghosts coming forward to haunt her mind, her worries about herself, her life, her thesis, but what he said next chased them all away.

"Those things you said in your email? About having to be one way for everyone else? That's bullshit. You're amazing just how you are. You can be the mathematician and the hiker, the brilliant M.I.T. student and the girl I fuck on dining room tables."

She laughed, but it was a sound of pain and relief, one that started in her lungs and broke somewhere around her heart.

Connor stroked her cheek and wiped away the tear that streaked down her face.

"You can be all those things, Gabby. Duality isn't a bad thing. It's the different sides of us that make us who we are. It makes us whole."

She gazed at him, at this man who in a week made everything she'd ever doubted about herself disappear. She blinked, feeling the different pieces of her life fall into place, and suddenly, she knew what she had to do. Wriggling out of his embrace, she hopped up off the bed and reached for her computer, sitting back down to open it on her knees. Connor sat up behind her.

"What are you doing?"

"Emailing my advisor. I need to tell him I'm reversing the direction of my thesis."

"You are?"

She turned over his shoulder to see his perfect face blooming into a grin. "Yeah, I think I am."

She couldn't disprove the Duality Principle anymore. It made no sense. It was illogical to even try. Because she could be both A and B, could love both the rose and its thorns. She could be the butterfly and break out of the ugly casing the caterpillar wove, letting love and nature turn her into something beautiful. She could be Gabby Evans, the mathematician and the freaky slut, and give in to the dual sides of her being. She could be true to who she was, just as her grandmother said she should, and let both sides shine.

Proving that duality existed was undeniable—she couldn't refute it anymore—especially as Connor hooked his finger in her shirt and drew her back down beside him into her bed.

THIRTEEN

Connor pulled on his helmet and straddled his bike. August was closing in around him. He could feel it from inside his riding jacket—the humidity already a little less noticeable, the season coming to an end. Tourists were still everywhere, desperate in their attempts to enjoy what remained of summer until the back-to-school signs herded them home.

Connor felt the same desperation too.

He knocked back the kickstand with one leg and cranked the Yamaha to life. The four-cylinders purred into action under him, just like he'd known they would when he rebuilt it.

The guy who'd nearly destroyed this beautiful machine didn't know shit about bikes. It had probably been a midlife crisis purchase, a whim he'd gone and spent fourteen grand on in an attempt to feel young again. He'd brought it into the shop, banged up and on the back of a flatbed. The engine had seized on the ramp to 95 and that's when it rolled. Jerry, Connor's boss, promised the guy he had the best mechanics in Portland, but the owner didn't care about fixing it. He just wanted to know how much it was worth.

Connor brought the Yamaha into the back. He'd never loved the bikes he worked on, but this one spoke to him somehow. It was a year out of the dealership at most, with smooth lines, charcoal black from end to end. A more thorough inspection proved that the engine wasn't busted but had probably been raced down the street before the oil had a chance to warm up, still thick and cold and unable to do its job. The dipshit out front had taken crappy care of it, never even did so much as an oil change. There was some corrosion too, but that was common in coastal areas because of all the sea salt in the air. The scratches were minor, something that could be fixed with some chrome polish and elbow grease. It would need work, but it wasn't trashed.

He'd gone out front and given Jerry his analysis: internal damage, scored main bearings, a shitload of valves bent. Even in good condition, it would have depreciated to half its worth, but with the engine rebuild and other work needing to be done, they should take another two grand off the top. It was obvious the owner had lost his taste for riding, though, and just wanted to be rid of it. It wasn't much of a surprise that when Jerry threw a number at him that wasn't even in the ballpark of reality, the guy went for it.

Connor started working on it right away. The bike reminded him a little of himself—beaten up, taken care of by someone who had no business riding it and then rejected. He needed to fix that bike, needed to see it returned to its former glory. He came in early when he didn't have class, worked past his afternoon shift late into the night. Once the rebuild was done, he took it out for a test. It didn't make any horrible noises and accelerated decently enough to make him happy with his work. But it seemed hard to let the handlebars go when he rumbled back into the shop, and Jerry had known the look in his eyes right away.

He put it on layaway for Connor. Slivers of his paycheck

went to keeping it under a tarp in the back of the garage. The summer before he met Gabby, the bike was finally his.

Connor slid his boots onto the footrests, found his balance and sped off. Now he knew what his father had felt when he was riding—the freedom, the heady exhilaration. It made him understand Travis a little better when the Yamaha went from stationary to sixty in two-point-eight flat. He eased back, taking it easy on the throttle since he didn't have far to go. Harnessing the bike's energy, however, was almost as hard as tapping into the control he needed for what was happening tonight. And for tomorrow too.

His stomach tightened in anticipation of where he'd be this time tomorrow, with the dinner hour in front of him and Gabby on her way back to Cambridge.

They'd had an amazing summer together after that crazy, confusing first week. It seemed like years ago, after all the things they'd packed into the weeks that followed. She'd been busy reworking her thesis, and Connor had used the time while she was working to read up on search engine optimization, enjoying the quiet of her grandmother's house and watching Gabby think. She talked to herself sometimes, especially when trying to reason something out. It was one of her little quirks he'd come to adore, one of the many things that made air catch in his chest at the same time as blood rushed down to his dick. He'd had to practice the art of patience more times than he could count, letting her work when he'd much rather have been working *her* over.

To be honest, they'd done plenty of that too. It hadn't taken him long to figure out she had a thing for doing it in places they might get caught. He could have kicked himself for misreading all the signs she was giving him in the beginning. He'd made up for it, though, against the windows of her bedroom, in her car, and even once on her front porch after finding some creative positioning and a blanket to cover them up. At the first beach bonfire party they'd gone to together, she'd sat down between his legs and leaned back against him, her hand snaking back behind her, nails scraping over the zipper of his fly. He'd hissed and hauled her up from the sand, ignoring the way Jamie and Dean smirked at them as he led Gabby to the abandoned lifeguard stand.

He still remembered the way her legs felt wrapped around him that night, the way her fingers dug into his back, and him unable to keep his eyes open, clutching the slatted wood they were braced against, something more powerful than an orgasm taking over him.

He was sure he'd never forget how she carried herself at dinner with his grandparents the week after that, either, with a poise that so easily covered the bad girl underneath. Or maybe it wasn't a cover. Maybe it was just Gabby, both angel and devil, never all one or the other, and Connor enjoyed getting to be both sides of himself with her too—proper when necessary and letting loose when they were alone.

His grandparents loved her, of course, and Connor thought he might feel the same way, although that wasn't a word he and Gabby ever exchanged. Wondering if he loved her, and if it was possible she felt the same way about him, was what helped propel his doubts along during their other adventures. She'd said she wanted to feel the open road like he did and asked him to ride them out to a hike in the White Mountains. They'd gone to Jerry's and Connor showed her all the body armor she'd need. Seeing her in a riding jacket and gloves nearly had him rubbing one off in the shop's dingy bathroom. She looked damn good in leather and even hotter when she topped it off with a helmet. He decided to upgrade his helmet too, and insisted on paying for both of them, splurging on a matched set with Bluetooth integration so they could talk during the ride.

They'd set out early one Saturday morning, her voice in his

ear, arms tight around his waist as she marveled over the quality of the helmet, how it channeled the air around her head. She said she'd always wondered how he'd stopped from getting dehydrated in the heat. He'd replied something about soaking his shirt under his clothes and the brilliance of his grandfather's advice on showers, but talking about being naked and wet with Gabby while he was supposed to be focusing on the road was a formula for disaster. It was already difficult enough to concentrate with her body pressed against his back, her legs split open on either side of him. He had to pull over, had to insist on changing into the bathing suits they'd stashed in her backpack. He'd carried her laughing into the crisp, cool mountain run-off that cut a rocky path between Lincoln and Conway, warming her with his body over hers and his hand down her bikini. It was either that or they'd both have become smudges somewhere on the Kancamagus Highway.

They'd come back to his house later that evening to find it empty. A note from his grandparents had been left on the dining room table saying they'd gone down to Ogunquit for an impromptu overnight getaway.

"You can hop in the shower if you want," he told her. "I need to clean the drive chain."

"I'll wait. I want to watch."

"Seriously? It's pretty basic. And kind of sticky and messy too."

She'd smiled coyly and followed him back into the garage. "Fine by me."

Connor chuckled. Only Gabby could turn something as grime-filled and boring as oiling a chain into something hot and sexy. She settled herself onto the floor while he set the bike up on its stand. He peeled off his riding jacket and shirt, changing into one of the ratty tanks he wore for greasy jobs before bending down and starting to work. He could feel Gabby's eyes on him, and he smirked. The shirt made his arms look good and he knew it.

"Any idea why it's best to lube after a ride, not before?" he asked her.

"I would have thought it would be the other way around."

"No, you do it after because then the chain is nice and hot. The lube penetrates better into the links that way."

"Penetrate," she said.

He turned to grin at her. "That's what I said." The words were innocent enough, but he could see them affecting her already, through the quickening of her breaths and the way her eyes changed. Fuzzy, drunk with lust.

She got up on her knees and crawled closer to him. Connor felt himself thicken, hardening for her despite how, only hours before, she'd had her fingers wrapped around him in the water. Crazy, the shit this girl could do to him.

"Anything else you want to—" she bit his earlobe, "—penetrate?"

"Maybe. What did you have in mind?"

She moved in close. He could feel her hot breath over the span of his shoulder. Then she bent low and sparked her tongue out over his bicep, licking slowly across his tattoo. He groaned. The chain could wait.

With grease still on his fingers, he stripped her down. She didn't mind the way he ran an oily line between her breasts, painting her in the markings of his past, or how he left handprints behind on her sides when he stopped to pull a condom from his pocket. She'd taken the reins then, yanked down his pants and boxers, and climbed on top of him. She even took his dirty hands in hers and dragged them back to her hips, silently asking him to guide her movements, to set the pace. He'd complied, happy to take the chill of the cement floor against his back if it meant he got to watch Gabby writhe above him, to feel her tighten when she got close and hear her tiny gasps when she got even closer. He arched up and fisted his hand in her hair, knowing exactly what it would take to push her to the edge, and swallowed her moans with a kiss that took him over as well.

She was still trembling when he'd picked her up and sat her down on the bike, her long legs splayed out on either side of it, back slippery against the leather. She tried to shimmy away from him when he started to play with her clit, saying she was too sensitive to go again, but he knew she could. He knew her body, knew all its cues. Her eyes slid closed and that crush of emotion he'd felt at the bonfire returned—a compression that seemed to force its way through him from the inside out. It was a need to be closer, to solder his bond to her. To quiet the doubts that told him these adventures they were having were no more than just that. That Gabby didn't think he was the best thing that ever happened to her, because if she did, how could he ever believe her? She was still the kind of girl who went beyond his wildest expectations. The kind he still thought he could never have. She hadn't mentioned anything about what was going to happen after the summer ended, and the thought of her leaving wrecked him so thoroughly he almost couldn't breathe.

She'd pulsed against his fingers, and he'd squeezed his eyes shut, mouthing the words *I love you.*

Connor sped around the corner and found Gabby waiting outside her grandmother's house. She'd thought it wasn't going to be hers to stay in much longer, but tonight was going to change all that. She turned toward him as he pulled up on the driveway, her riding gear on, helmet balanced against her hip.

He flipped up his visor. "You ready?"

She tucked an envelope into the inside pocket of her jacket and zipped it up. "Hell yeah."

She climbed on behind him, and he could feel her energy, her excitement. He'd almost seen that light go out in her the week before, when her parents had called, telling her an interested buyer had put an offer on the house, and they were overnighting some paperwork for her to sign. It was a proviso in her grandmother's will, stipulating that if a decision were made to sell the house, everyone in the family would have to be in agreement about it, including Gabby.

She'd never known the clause existed before. She hadn't signed it. She hadn't told her parents that when they'd come up today to finalize the deal with the buyer, either.

Connor put a little more kick in the engine as they flew past the restaurant where her parents were waiting, hoping they heard the buzz and wrinkled their disapproving, holier-than-thou noses at it. He found a spot halfway up the block, and Gabby shook her hair out of her helmet but didn't look at him. She was steeling herself, pulling down the gates and rolling up the drawbridge to her emotions. He knew she was only doing it so she didn't get hurt. Hell, he'd done it himself a million times before, but he didn't like it. He had so little time left with her, and he wanted to spend it with her shining.

He took her hand in his and squeezed.

Inside the restaurant, her parents were waiting at a table by the window. Her hand tightened around his when her mother zeroed in on them, gawking as she took Connor in, from his boots to his helmet-mussed hair. Gabby had told them she was bringing someone to dinner, and her mother had apparently been ecstatic at another prospect for a suitable husband, but it was obvious she didn't like what she saw. Connor wanted to grin and say, *That's right, I'm the one your daughter's been with all summer*, but this wasn't his night to be the rebel. It was Gabby's.

"Hi," she said when they reached the table. Her father skirted his gaze over the edge of the menu then looked back down at it, just as Gabby had predicted. God, these people were such shits.

"Who's this?" her mother asked. She looked a little like

Gabby, with the same blonde hair, although Connor had a feeling at her age, the color came out of the bottle. Her mouth was the same shape as Gabby's too, but thinner and meaner-looking, her lips pressed into a sneer.

"This is Connor. My boyfriend."

She'd never put it that way before, even though it had pretty much been implied, and he stood up a little taller and smiled. He couldn't help it.

Gabby pulled out a chair and sat. "Since you've made so many comments about me never being satisfied, I thought you'd want to meet the man that is finally...satisfying me."

She looked up at Connor and grinned. That pressure in his chest made full impact again, but he breathed through it, winked and sat down next to her.

"I assume you've brought the paperwork?" her father asked, still flipping through the menu. "You've had it notarized?"

"As a matter of fact, I haven't."

That got his attention. "You haven't," he repeated.

"Nope." Gabby popped the P at the end of the word. Connor had to stifle his laugh.

"Gabriella," her mother said. Connor watched Gabby stiffen at the name. "Explain yourself."

Gabby unzipped her jacket and took the envelope out of the pocket. She held it in her hands before looking back up at them. "Have you known about this since Nana died? The clause about the whole family agreeing?"

"Of course we did," her mother answered.

Gabby shook her head and laughed. It was a sad sound, one Connor hadn't heard much over the past few weeks. He recognized it from earlier in the summer, from when she was still struggling between the idea of who she was and who she thought she had to be.

She laid the envelope on the table. "I'm not signing it."

Her mother's eyes blazed. "We are meeting the buyer tomorrow, Gabriella. Yes, you certainly are going to—"

But then Gabby's father put a hand out, silencing her. Her mother looked stunned but stayed quiet as Mr. Evans calmly placed his menu down on the plate and asked, "Why?"

There didn't seem to be any anger in his voice. Only genuine curiosity.

Gabby looked at her lap and rubbed her palms over her jeans. Connor linked his hands together to stop himself from touching her, from comforting her.

"How could you..." she began then stopped herself, swallowing hard. Lifting her head, she met her father's gaze. "How could you not know how much that house means to me? How much I loved being there with Nana, every summer you brought me here. When now that she's gone—"

Her voice broke, and she bit her lip. This time, Connor did reach over to her and covered the fingers that were gripping her jeans with his palm.

I'm here.

You can do this.

"When now that's she's gone, it's all that's left of her."

There was a long moment of uneasy silence. Connor watched Gabby's father consider her words, his gaze fixed on something in the corner of the room. Then he looked back at her. Connor swore he saw something different than what she'd said was in his distant gazes. Something that looked like respect.

"I had no idea the house meant so much to you." He took the envelope from the table, folded it once and put it in his breast pocket. "We'll back out of the deal with the buyers tomorrow and take it off the market. You can stay there as long as you like."

Her mother opened and closed her mouth but said nothing. Connor watched Gabby exhale in relief, the color coming back to her face. She beamed and turned her hand over in his, giving it a tight squeeze.

"Thanks, Dad," she said. "Thank you so much."

It wasn't quite a happily ever after for them, but it was a start.

When dinner was over, they rode back through the streets of Portland. Connor insisted on a little victory lap, hoping Gabby would just enjoy the ride and not pay too much attention to where they were going. He drove them past the coffee shop where they'd met, then the ice cream parlor. He picked up speed on Commercial, passing the wharves where fewer boats now rocked in their slips than in early July. The sun had already set by the time they went over the Casco Bay Bridge, the air laced with just a touch of pre-autumn chill, but he took the long way around anyway, threading through South Portland to Bug Light Park, then by the tavern at SMCC. By the time he pulled up in front of her grandmother's house, he had to swallow around the lump in his throat.

He needed to get his act together. He had lots of plans on how they were going to spend their last night here, and none of them included him crying.

"Can you believe it?" she asked, pulling him up the walkway and inside. She paused in the entryway and closed her eyes. "I can't believe I get to keep this house."

"I believe it." He stepped in close behind her and folded her in his arms. Breathed in the smell of her hair and kissed the top of her head. "I'm so proud of you."

"Come on." She broke away from him and reached back to circle her fingers around his wrist. "I need to finish packing."

She sounded almost giddy. He was happy for her, but the hollowness in his stomach made his feet drag as he followed her up the steps to her bedroom. She started transferring clothes from her drawers into an open suitcase, kneeling on the floor next to it.

She'd already packed so much, the room looked almost empty. Connor sat on the edge of the bed and folded his hands.

"Okay, my first holiday is in two weeks. I can drive back here for that," she said. "The next one isn't until Columbus Day, but I'll need to come back to check on the house before then, to make sure it's set for winter. I'm off for Veteran's Day, and then it's Thanksgiving. I know that doesn't seem like a lot, so here."

She stood up and handed him a small envelope.

"What's this?"

"A gift. And a bribe." She plopped down next to him. "Open it."

He pulled the flap open. Inside were two tickets to at least half a dozen Red Sox home games.

"I can't...you shouldn't have..." Connor sighed. "This must have cost you fortune."

She snuggled up close to him. "Well, they're for me too. Sort of. I mean, I'm not really into baseball, but I still have tons of fantasies of all these raunchy things I'd love you to do to me around campus. This is just a reason to get you to come to Cambridge."

As if he needed a bribe for that. He wanted to say something about being into every filthy thing she could come up with, that he had every intention of making her fantasies a reality, but there was that pressure again. Connor rubbed his chest and took a shaky breath, trying to talk, but he couldn't bring himself to ask her if this was more than just sex. If this summer meant as much to her as it did to him. He'd sound like a pussy, and he wasn't sure what kind of answer he wanted to hear.

"Anyway," she continued. "I'll probably be a wreck over Thanksgiving because my thesis is due pretty much right when I get back, and I'll be even worse until my defense is over. But the semester ends a few days before Christmas, and assuming it gets accepted, all I'll have to do is prep it for publication in January. Then I'm done. And I'll be here."

"Wait, you don't have to go back to school?"

"Not until my hooding ceremony in June."

"And you'll be staying in Portland."

She looked at him like he'd gone slightly insane. "Of course. I've already started looking for jobs. I saw an opening coming up for an assistant professor at the University of Southern Maine's Department of Math and Stats and thought I'd apply."

Connor looked down at the tickets in his hand as relief and uncertainty coiled their way through him, tugging him in opposite directions. It was what he wanted, more than anything, but he didn't want her coming back to Maine for him, to live out what might become a future of disgruntled hopes, when, just like his mother, she might have been able to accomplish so much more. Wasn't this what love was? Letting it go and hoping it came back to you, or some shit like that?

"Are you sure that's the right choice?" he asked. "I mean, it's not very logical to make decisions on the rest of your life based on two months with me."

"Screw logic. I love Portland. I love this house. And I love you."

The weight on his chest grew heavier and then somehow snapped. His eyes found hers, but even when his mouth opened, no words would come.

"Since I met you, nothing has made sense," she told him. "Nothing has been logical, ordered or defined. But at the same time, everything has made perfect sense. You can't get more duality than that." Her grin grew wide. "Maybe I should write a paper on how blind dates really can go well, despite the statistics."

"I love you too," he blurted out, then grimaced and looked away.

"I know. I've known all summer."

He chanced a gaze back up at her. She was smiling big and bright, her gray eyes sparkling behind her glasses.

She pointed to her head. "I'm smart *and* outdoorsy, remember?"

He laughed but ducked his eyes down again. Despite her finally saying the words he'd wanted to hear, he couldn't reply, couldn't fight back the fears that had plagued him all his life. That someone he loved would actually be coming back to him. Staying with him.

Gabby cupped his face in both her hands and drew his gaze up to hers.

"We're both geeks and rebels, you and me. The perfect match, balanced and mathematically sound." She rubbed her nose over his, a sweet, simple move that spoke of intimacies he'd never known. "Didn't you know by now that I loved you? You're the best thing that ever happened to me, Connor Starks."

And when she kissed him, Connor closed his eyes and finally believed her.

I hope you enjoyed *The Duality Principle*. Connor and Gabriella were complicated, stubborn, and intense to write, and I wouldn't have wanted them any other way.

If their push and pull hooked you, surprised you, or left you fanning yourself more than once, I'd love to hear what you thought. Reader reviews help books like this find new readers who enjoy sharp contrasts, real heat, and a love story that earns every moment.

If you feel like sharing, you can leave a review wherever you purchased the book, or on Goodreads. Even a few honest words make a real difference.

 *Rebecca Grace Allen*

ALSO BY REBECCA GRACE ALLEN

Legally Bound:

His Contract

Her Claim

Their Discovery

Portland Rebels:

The Hierarchy of Needs

The Theory of Deviance

Shakespeare in the City:

Taming Sugar

Hunter Pains

Decades Duet:

Find the Cost of Freedom

Smells Like Teen Spirit

EXCERPT FROM THE HIERARCHY OF NEEDS

"I think we're safe," he said. Jamie was too busy laughing to hear him.

She fell into a rounded booth in the corner and swung her legs up onto the middle of the cushion, her hands on her stomach as if it hurt to laugh. Her dress had inched up her thighs, the fabric clinging to her hips.

Hunger clawed at Dean at the sight of her body sprawled out like that. With her legs up on the seat, her head tossed back and her smile wide, she looked so relaxed. So free. So Jamie. He stopped at the edge of the table and stared at her legs, wanting so goddamn badly to be trapped between them, to finally be buried inside her, to feel her heat and watch her mouth drop open in pleasure.

What was he thinking? She was his friend. His *friend*. When was he going to get that through his skull?

Jamie finally stopped laughing. She sighed and smiled. "That. Was. Awesome."

"Yeah, you're pretty damn funny when you want to be."

Another giggle fizzled out of her. She looked ridiculously pleased with herself.

"We should probably lay low for a few," she said. "Until the rage gets out of Sean's system."

"Why do you do it?" he asked. "The jokes on your brothers."

He'd always found her prankster nature amusing, but never understood why she did it.

She shrugged. "Someone's gotta take them down a peg or two. Make them feel less like the gods they think they are."

There was more she was covering up, something other than sibling rivalry, but he couldn't get a handle on what it was.

"Are you just gonna stand there?" She patted the spot next to her. "Sit."

She lowered her legs and scooted over so he could join her. Dean held himself still, tension like a live wire inside him. It was as if every bone, every fiber in his body was dragging him forward, a magnet being pulled toward true north.

It wasn't a good idea, not only because she'd been drinking. It was because he *felt* it again—that fuse that always simmered beneath the surface between them, waiting for a spark.

It was a dangerous feeling. Dean didn't know if he had the power to resist it.

He sat down anyway. Jamie turned to face him, one elbow balanced on top of the seat cushion, her hand propping up her head. The motion put the soft, full curve of her breast into full view. Dean clenched his jaw and clasped his hands together on his lap.

"Thank you for helping out today," she said.

"No problem. I had fun." His mouth went dry. He swallowed. "Thank you for hiring me."

She grinned, her eyes drifting closed for a second, and Dean jumped at the chance to take her in. The rounded apples of her cheeks. Her neck and collarbones and the flat of her stomach. Her legs, curled up and pressed together beneath her.

He wondered if she still tasted the same.

"I didn't hire you, silly. I bribed you with food and beer, which I hope you enjoyed."

He didn't answer, too distracted when she turned to the side and toed off her heels, then got back into the same position. She'd moved closer to him while she did it, or maybe he'd been the one to move, he wasn't sure. All he knew was that he could feel the heat radiating off her, her body so close, all that gorgeous hair tumbling down over her shoulders.

He had to tighten his clasped fingers to the point of pain to stop himself from touching her. God, when had he started wanting her this badly?

His voice came out gritty when he said, "I had a good time anyway."

"I'm glad." Her eyes fell on his collar. "You look good in a suit."

Dean's pulse ratcheted up to full throttle. She brought a hand up to trace the edge of his neckline. Soft fingers stroked his neck.

He hissed in a breath. "Jamie."

It came out sounding like he was trying to stop her, like he realized what was about to happen and the mistake they were about to make all over again. A war raged between his head and his body, between the right thing to do and what he wanted, but Dean's ability to reason was hanging by a thread, and he couldn't make himself sure this was a mistake anymore.

She shook her head. "Don't talk." Pulling him to her, she whispered, "Just don't talk."

About the Author

Rebecca lives in southern Florida with three cats who firmly believe they are the main characters. When she's not immersed in fictional love stories, she can usually be found chasing strong coffee, good workouts, and the kind of books that balance heart, heat, and humor. She writes romance for readers who like their happily ever afters earned, their characters flawed, and their love stories a little messy in the best possible way.